"You feel so good, my love," Jim whispered.

"Your mouth...so hot, so sweet. Please, kiss me that way again."

And Sarah did, glorying in the furnace of his mouth as his probing tongue caused the blood to rush through her veins like licking flames. She wasn't thinking about Grant anymore. There was no time, no room for thought of anything but this moment, this man.

Locking her hands behind his neck, her fingers delighting in the feel of his skin, his hair, she let her tongue move eagerly over his lips, then on to explore his mouth. When she felt his hands move up under her sweater, however, she had the will to pull back. "We can't let this go any further," she said huskily.

Dear Reader:

Three months ago we were delighted to announce the arrival of TO HAVE AND TO HOLD, the thrilling new romance series that takes you into the world of married love. We're pleased to report that letters of praise and enthusiasm are pouring in daily. TO HAVE AND TO HOLD is clearly off to a great start!

TO HAVE AND TO HOLD is the first and only series that portrays the joys and heartaches of marriage. Its unique concept makes it significantly different from the other lines now available to you, and it presents stories that meet the high standards set by SECOND CHANCE AT LOVE. TO HAVE AND TO HOLD offers all the compelling romance, exciting sensuality, and heartwarming entertainment you expect.

We think you'll love TO HAVE AND TO HOLD—and that you'll become the kind of loyal reader who is making SECOND CHANCE AT LOVE an ever-increasing success. Read about love affairs that last a lifetime. Look for three TO HAVE AND TO HOLD romances each and every month, as well as six SECOND CHANCE AT LOVE romances each month. We hope you'll read and enjoy them all. And please keep writing! Your thoughts about our books are very important to us.

Warm wishes,

Ellen Edwards

Ellen Edwards
SECOND CHANCE AT LOVE
The Berkley Publishing Group
200 Madison Avenue
New York, N.Y. 10016

SHINING PROMISE

MARIANNE COLE

SECOND CHANCE AT LOVE
BOOK

Other Second Chance at Love books by
Marianne Cole

GENTLE AWAKENING   #101

SHINING PROMISE

Second Chance at Love books are published by
The Berkley Publishing Group
200 Madison Avenue, New York, NY 10016

CHAPTER ONE

WITH A GESTURE that wavered between annoyance and impatience, Sarah Harbison pushed back the long, dark strands of hair that clung damply to her forehead. The slender young woman with hazel eyes and delicate facial features shoved her hands into the pockets of her white sundress and continued to wander restlessly across Roger and Donna McKinnon's backyard. It was midway through August and hot days hadn't exactly been scarce in St. Louis, but this day was the hottest yet.

Given a choice, an outdoor family-style barbecue was not where Sarah would have spent the day. From what she could detect, everyone there was with someone . . . spouse, offspring, or both. Everyone, that is, except Sarah herself. She was here at the insistence

1

of Roger, a senior partner in the law firm Sarah had joined a few years ago—way back, when she was still married to Grant.

It was still not clear why Roger had insisted that she attend this picnic. Every woman she had met here had a child, was pregnant, or both. Conversation tended to center around methods of childbirth, brands of disposable diapers, day-care centers, and discipline methods. While Sarah had nothing against such conversations, she also had nothing to contribute. Her childless marriage had ended more than a year ago. She didn't even have any young nieces or nephews to talk about.

With wry amusement she noted that the talk about discipline was just that—talk. The children all seemed to be running wild and doing exactly as they pleased. Occasionally a mother would scream at a child to stop doing something, and when the child kept right on, the mother pretended not to notice. As the ice cubes in her glass of tea melted rapidly, Sarah listened with feigned fascination to tales of gifted and otherwise exceptional children and hoped her desperate need to escape did not show. She glanced over at Roger, who caught her eye and gave her a wide, impish grin. Apparently he was well aware of her feelings. With his thick thatch of silver hair, he looked like the distinguished attorney he was, even clad in shorts and a polo shirt. Murmuring an excuse, Sarah walked away from the cluster of women she had joined. If they noticed or cared, it didn't show.

The humidity registered higher than the temperature, and Sarah's cotton dress, so crisp and cool when she had put it on, now adhered to her flesh, making her feel uncomfortable and unkempt.

As she roamed aimlessly across the wide lawn, which was brown in patches from lack of rain, Sarah's attention focused on a man who hovered at the fringes of the crowd. He did not seem to belong at the McKinnons' evening barbecue any more than she did. Kindred spirits? she wondered. She judged him to be somewhat older than she, probably in his mid-thirties. He was extraordinarily good looking, despite a harried air. Tilting her head slightly, she gave him a keen appraisal: brown hair with a reddish tinge, strongly molded features, and without a spare ounce of flesh on his tall, muscular frame . . . yes, indeed, quite good looking.

The man lit a cigarette, took a drag on it, then exhaled. As if sensing that she was watching him, he turned and looked directly at her. His eyes were dark, perceptive, and commanding. When his gaze caught hers, it held. Perhaps Sarah could have broken that gaze. But she didn't want to. Meeting the eyes of a handsome stranger and feeling an inexplicable rapport with him . . . well, it just wasn't the sort of thing that happened to her. Not until now.

Sarah was not unaware that she was an attractive woman. She was used to men's attention. And yet, while she enjoyed that attention, she did not take such moments seriously or offer encouragement. At those times her protective mantle of reserve helped ward off those interested only in casual affairs and one-night stands.

This, however, was different. This indefinable ebb

and flow of silent communication. Sarah smiled despite herself and the man's eyes flickered, breaking the spellbound mood. He matched her smile with one of his own.

It was a nice smile, Sarah thought, and it lightened the burden of care mapped across his visage. Yet when he took a step toward her, she felt a surge of near panic. For a moment she wanted to turn and run away.

They had shared a bit of magic, but the reality of a meeting could only be a let-down. Undoubtedly he was married. He was someone else's husband, probably even someone else's husband on the prowl. How stupid of me, she fretted . . . now he's on the way over because he thinks I'm easy prey. Well, she had handled unwelcome advances before. Somewhat wistfully, however, she wished it hadn't come to this. She would have preferred to preserve the fairy tale moment in her memory, where she could draw on it on lonely nights, embroidering it with "what-if" fantasies.

Stopping in front of her, he said, "You look as out of place as I feel." His voice was firm and resonant.

"And I was trying so hard not to let it show," Sarah replied lightly, belying the pounding of her heart. Whatever her head was telling her, her soul was still caught up in the spell of make-believe.

"Oh, you're doing all the right things," he assured her. "I've watched you off and on since you got here. You seem to be walking through a world that isn't real to you."

"You're very perceptive."

He shrugged, muscles rippling beneath his yellow polo shirt. "Maybe I merely recognized your feeling because it's one I share. I hate these things."

Raising one eyebrow, she said, "You don't strike me as the sort of man accustomed to doing things you don't want to do."

Again he shrugged, then he field-stripped his cigarette, which had burned out, and finding no ashtray, put the butt in his back pocket. "Somehow Roger and Donna managed to convince me it would be good for Christina. Perhaps they're right. She, at least, seems to be enjoying herself. So I suppose we all do things we don't want to for the sake of those we love."

His deep brown eyes wandered from where they had rested on Sarah's face. Without being too obvious, she tried to follow the line of his gaze. Though she told herself it couldn't possibly matter, she wanted to see the woman who was worthy of such sacrifice. But there were too many people. Sarah couldn't pick out Christina. And, she told herself, it didn't matter anyway.

"Then why am I here?" Sarah murmured, almost unconsciously. "There's no one here I love."

"No?" he asked, scrutinizing her closely again.

"No," she echoed flatly, though for an insane moment her heart whispered, I thought I could love you.

"I'm glad to hear it. I know that must sound selfish, but the truth is . . ."

So here it comes, she thought wearily. The married man making his first move. What would his story be? Was Christina a nag, immature, an extravagant spender, frigid . . . all the above? Whatever her problems she was undoubtedly incapable of understanding his wants and needs, poor man.

Before Sarah could respond with appropriate sar-
casm, a small girl zoomed in out of nowhere and threw
herself at the man, hugging his knees with great enthusiasm. "There you are, Daddy. You promised me
you'd come watch me swim and I waited and waited
and you never did come."

"Never did come?" he repeated, laughing fondly.
"It's only been ten minutes since you asked me. I was
going to come in just a little bit. Now, don't I always
do what I promise, hm?"

"Yes, but..." The child's lower lip stuck out in a
pretty pout.... "Mrs. McKinnon says we have to clear
the pool soon and dry off because the food's almost
ready, so if you don't come now, you won't get to
see me swim at all. Please, Daddy?"

"Well, I certainly can't miss seeing you swim, can
I, Christy? Will you join us, Ms—?"

Sarah let the implied question go unanswered.
Shaking her head, she murmured her excuses and
edged away. Let him find the child's mother and they
could watch the child swim together.

Nodding, speaking, smiling—never pausing long
enough to enter a conversation—Sarah found her way
across the lawn. Her only desire was to find her hostess, make some excuse, and get away. Her mood had
run full circle and she, who always tried to be candid
with herself, felt like a fool. Thirty-one years old,
and here she was weaving fantasies around a man who
had chanced to catch her eye. Adolescent nonsense,
she thought furiously. Even more infuriating was the
surge of disappointment she experienced when the
fantasy turned sour.

She decided to view the brief encounter as a warning. Since her marriage to Grant Farrell had ended, she'd had little contact with eligible men. This was due partly to choice and partly to the scarcity of such men. She had accepted a few dates and had been trapped into others by well-meaning friends. None of the men had interested her. Ruefully, she had observed that there were few men who were secure enough to feel at ease dating a dedicated attorney-at-law. She loved her work, and yet she had to admit it did little to salve her loneliness.

Never a single-faceted person, Sarah acknowledged with a sudden burst of honesty that she was bored. It was true! Outside of the law office, the courtroom, there didn't seem to be any place she fit. Not having a family, she felt out of place at picnics like this. And she positively loathed cocktail parties, bridge clubs, and organized women's social groups.

When she wasn't spending sixteen hours a day working, she filled her spare time with reading, jogging, and doing volunteer work at a large children's hospital. Occasionally she had lunch or went shopping with a woman friend. An exciting life, she thought wistfully. No wonder she was so vulnerable to fantasy. But now that she was aware of the danger, all she had to do was keep that amber warning light flashing. Although she had not ruled out the possiblity of remarriage, she had vowed never again to be fooled by a shiny surface. Next time she would take the time to know a man thoroughly before getting involved.

She had just passed the bar exam when she met Grant Farrell. Swept off her feet by his charm and attentiveness, it hadn't taken Sarah long to realize she didn't know her husband. She had married his public image, had fallen for his carefully prepared publicity hype. What she eventually learned of the real Grant Farrell came as quite a shock. But no more, she thought ruefully, than her true nature had come as a shock to him.

Grant had wooed and won a pretty dark-haired woman who complemented his own appearance well, an intelligent, educated, photogenic, and soft-spoken woman. She was expected to be his hostess and companion at an endless round of social functions designed to advance his political ambitions.

"But, Grant, I'm a lawyer too," she had protested. "I can never build a career if I don't devote time to it."

He answered such declarations by patting her shoulder and smiling indulgently. It didn't bother him that she was a lawyer. Actually, he thought it made a fine hobby for her . . . a hobby he viewed as having no more importance than needlepoint or golf. He had delivered many eloquent speeches backing women's rights, and yet he was constant in his private battle to get his wife to sacrifice her career. He wanted her to devote her time and energy to his career.

Snapping out of this reverie about her broken marriage, Sarah sought out Donna McKinnon in the kitchen. "Donna, I hate to run off before we've even eaten, but . . ."

"But what, Sarah dear?" Donna asked, narrowing her eyes. Donna was in her forties, her skin bronzed and leathery from hours of golf and tennis at the country club.

"I don't feel too well," Sarah said feebly. "I guess it's just that this oppressive heat is getting to me."

"There's a bottle of aspirin right over there on the cabinet," the older woman replied. "Take a couple of those and you'll be good as new. Now, come on, help me carry these salads out to the tables."

"Donna . . ."

Donna McKinnon turned from the counter where she was fussing with arranging tomato wedges and deviled eggs on a platter. "Besides, Sarah, Roger would kill us both if I let you get away before dinner. Chin up, dear!"

With a resigned sigh, Sarah reached for the aspirin, took two tablets, and began to help. As soon as possible, she was going to find Roger and pin him down on why exactly he thought it was so important that she be here.

Once she'd begun to help with the meal, it was hard to stop. In fact, Sarah found she greatly preferred carrying bowls and seeing that all the dishes had serving spoons or forks to seeking out a group to sit with. At Donna's insistence, she nibbled at some food as she worked. She really felt too hot and depressed to have much of an appetite.

Looking over the flock of artfully placed picnic tables, she again found the handsome dark-haired stranger. The little girl danced around at his side, happy with a hot dog in one hand and a bottle of soda pop in the other. If a woman belonged with them, Sarah couldn't tell which one it might be. Most of the women here were like Donna, though their sizes and ages varied. Their husbands were affluent professional men; few of these wives worked. Most seemed to spend the summer taking care of kids and getting a tan. Somehow that didn't seem to fit with the dark-haired man. Sarah wasn't sure why. At any rate, no one had materialized at his side.

"What are you thinking about? You seem a million miles away," Donna remarked as she bustled by.

Sarah flushed slightly, doubting that Donna would be flattered by her thoughts. Then she grinned. "It's just heat stroke," she said. "Your fault. You should have let me go home."

"Nonsense," Donna countered. "Now, be a dear and go see if the Marshalls need anything. They wouldn't ask for the world, but they are up in years and a bit arthritic."

Sarah approached the elderly couple. Gratefully, they accepted her offer to bring them something. Weaving through the tables as she performed her various tasks, Sarah felt eyes on her. She didn't have to look to know to whom those eyes belonged. Brushing by his table once, she couldn't help meeting his gaze. At that moment, the child took a wide sweep with the hot dog and it made close contact with her father's shirt. Smiling at Sarah, he wiped away most of the damage with a paper napkin. "Now you know why I wore a yellow shirt—to camouflage the mustard."

And still no bronzed young matron by his side, she noted. Sarah returned the man's smile, but made no reply.

A few moments later, when the desserts had been put on display and the McKinnons' guests were crowding around to make their selections, Sarah looked down to see little auburn-haired Christy staring sadly at the table. She held an empty paper plate.

"Is the dessert you wanted gone?" Sarah asked the child.

Christy shook her head, eyes flitting back and forth between a large chocolate cake and a cream-whipped strawberry confection. "I can't make up my mind," she said wistfully.

"Take both," Sarah urged. "There's plenty. I'm sure Mrs. McKinnon won't mind."

"I can't," Christy confided. "Daddy said I could have *one* dessert and that's all."

"I see." Sarah looked at the cake and the strawberry dessert, both cut in generous, adult-sized portions. "They do both look delicious, don't they?"

The child nodded solemnly, eyes growing bigger by the moment.

On impulse, Sarah said, "I don't know which to take either. Why don't we share?"

Christy seemed unsure that she trusted Sarah enough to enter into such a conspiracy.

"Look," Sarah explained. "I'll cut a piece of each in two. That way, we'll both have some of each. And it still won't be having more than one dessert, because two halves are a whole. Do you see?"

Smiling brightly, Christy held out her plate. With a quick flick of the serving knife, Sarah placed half a piece of cake and half a serving of the strawberry fluff onto the child's paper plate. Still hesitant about the situation, Christy waited around to make sure Sarah put the remaining halves on her own plate.

"I'm sure your father won't mind," Sarah assured

her. "Lots of people share foods this way so they can try different things without wasting or overeating. He just didn't think of suggesting it, I'm sure."

Christy went back to join her father. Sarah watched with amusement while the child, gesturing and speaking rapidly, explained how she had ended up with two desserts. If he objected it was not evident, for the child nestled herself onto his lap while she ate.

When the meal was over, the talk grew lazier, and as time ticked by, the sun was less intense. Sarah was now determined to make her getaway. She had given up on cornering Roger. He could explain himself on Monday morning. But as she moved to go, she suddenly found her path blocked by Christy's father. She couldn't help smiling when she saw the front of his expensive shirt. The mustard smears had been joined by chocolate frosting, whipped cream, and strawberry syrup. Knowing she should keep her reserve and pass by with a civil nod, she laughed despite herself. "Yellow wasn't such a good idea after all. Plaid might've been better!"

"You're definitely right. How on earth did you manage to keep that white dress so spotless?"

Sarah looked down at the white pique and thought that no child had nestled there; perhaps she wouldn't have minded a few spots and stains. What she said was, "I guess I just stood well back from things and was very careful."

"Something tells me, Sarah Harbison, that standing well back from things and being careful is not unusual for you. Perhaps it's even a way of life."

She looked at him in surprise. What a presumptuous statement! She supposed she should be offended, yet he didn't seem to have meant anything by it, for he was looking at her guilelessly. "You know my name," she said. "I can't remember mentioning it." And if I'd met you before, she mused, I would have remembered.

"You didn't," he said. "Roger told me about you. He said when I found a dark-haired woman with the face of a Raphael madonna and the body of Venus, I'd know I'd found Sarah Harbison. Why he didn't simply introduce us is beyond me, but I've known Roger for years and he has his own means and methods."

Lights of understanding flashed on in Sarah's head. Then this entire scheme was nothing more than her boss's attempt at matchmaking. Aware of her stubborn streak and her intense dislike of blind dates, Roger had hinted that her required presence had something to do with business. Clever, she admitted. And if he were matchmaking, then this man must not be married. She tried to ignore, or at least discount, the flow of pleasure she experienced as she digested that idea.

"The face of a madonna and the body of Venus?" she asked dryly. "I didn't know Roger ever looked at me that closely."

"Show me a man who wouldn't look at you and I'll call the morgue to come pick him up."

"Listen to that. And I don't even know your name. It makes me wonder how flowery the compliments get on better acquaintance."

His laughter rang out. It was a nice laugh that fit with the rest of him.

"I'm really not much on that sort of thing. Roger said it. And I did find you, based on his description. But I can't say I agree with it entirely."

"Oh?"

"Madonnas on canvas. Statues carved of stone. Art has its place. But it's only an imitation of life."

Sarah shook her head in mock dismay. "For someone who claims not to be much on that sort of thing, you do rather well. A little practice and you can try for your sharpshooter's badge."

"Doubt my sincerity?"

"I don't know you well enough to express doubt or belief. Which brings me back to the fact that you still haven't told me who you are. Roger certainly told you more than he told me—I was simply ordered to show up."

"He didn't tell you?"

Sarah shrugged, turning her palms upward. "Nothing. Not a hint."

His smile was hard to read. "Well, I suppose I should fill you in then. Do you have a few minutes? I've got to take my daughter home soon. But maybe we can grab a cool drink and sit down somewhere first."

Feeling almost mesmerized, Sarah followed the man, who, she noted, had not yet divulged his name. He led her toward an old-fashioned wooden swing which hung by ropes from a huge oak tree.

Once they were seated, he looked at her squarely. "I'm Jim Laney," he announced. His pause gave the impression this should have some meaning to her. Searching frantically through her mind, Sarah decided the name did have a familiar ring. All she had to do was associate it with something.

Right hand on the rope, left arm stretched out across the back of the swing, he was impossibly attractive...all sinewy muscle and an aura of overpowering masculinity.

Swings were where lovers sat on dark nights to watch the stars. Looking heavenward, Sarah saw that a few stars had made it out. Although she told herself sternly that romantic environments were to be avoided with a man she didn't know, the stars stayed obstinately in place.

"Quit trying to figure out who I am," he said at last. "When you go back to work on Monday, you'll find my name down for two o'clock on your appointment log."

Sarah immediately cancelled out her previous thoughts and let another set of thoughts move in. Folding her hands in her lap almost primly, she said, "Then this is business."

His gaze swept over her face in the dimly lit yard. "That's true. After meeting you, though, I regret it very much. Roger must have a sadistic streak. He advises me against romantic adventures and then puts me in contact with the loveliest woman I've seen in years."

She sat up straighter in the swing, back braced by the wooden slats. Thoughts of fairy-tale romance evaporated completely. "I remember now. Roger told me about a friend who wanted to sue for custody of his child. He told me some of the facts, and I had reservations. I suppose that's why he insisted I come today.

To see you with the child. He wanted to arouse my sympathy."

"And did he?"

Sarah smiled. "We'll need more than sympathy to build a case. Any parent who is separated from his children hurts. Such are the perils of divorce. Christy is a sweet kid, cute, and very well mannered for her age."

"Only at times," he replied with a laugh. "At others she's a perfect model for a frightful four. Are you familiar with Dr. Spock? Probably not. But if it'll put sympathy in my corner, I'll tell you that you made quite an impression on her. She referred to you as 'that nice, pretty lady.'"

"As I've said, we'll need more than sympathy. Why do you want me to represent you, Mr. Laney?"

"Jim," he corrected.

She nodded, then watched silently while he squirmed uncomfortably. He fished a package of cigarettes from his pocket. When he offered her one, she told him she didn't smoke.

"I'm in the process of quitting," he told her. "A few weeks ago I was a chain smoker. Now I'm down to half a pack a day or less. Actually, it was Christy's idea. She asked why I smoked. I didn't have a good answer, so I decided to quit."

"You seem to be a very determined man. I'm sure you can quit if you put your mind to it. However, you didn't answer my question."

"That's the lawyer in you—you won't let a man sidestep an issue. Actually, I was going to answer, but the question made me so nervous, I needed a cigarette."

"That bad?"

"Well, Sarah, the truth is I didn't exactly want you to represent me. I asked Roger to do it. He said I'd stand a better chance with you, that it would look good in court to have a female on my side. So, since you and I both had reservations, he brought us together informally at the barbecue."

Christina chose that moment to seek them out, talked shyly for a few moments, then settled down between Sarah and Jim on the swing, leaning her head against his shoulder.

"And your reservations were . . ." Sarah said, picking up the thread of their conversation.

He paused, then offered her a sheepish grin. "I suppose my reasoning goes back to the feudal days, but I felt I'd be more comfortable dealing with Roger or another male attorney. I'm sure you find that attitude offensive."

Sarah shrugged. Although not a militant feminist, she had never appreciated having her capabilities questioned on the basis of her sex. "I suppose I've learned to live with that attitude," she said finally. "My grandfather was a lawyer. When I was a child, he thought it was cute that I was so intrigued by his office and books. Yet when I told him I wanted to be a lawyer, he thought I'd lost my mind. None of my family really approved. But it was what I wanted, and I went after it. I realize some clients will shy away, but a growing number of people actively seek out a female attorney. That doesn't please me either. I'd rather see people choosing legal counsel on the basis of reputation and capability. But we all just do the best we can."

"I gather you like your work, then."

"Very much."

"Don't write me off as a chauvinist, Sarah. Christy has a book called *Girls Can Do Anything*—or something like that. I even read it to her. In fact, I certainly hope that when she grows up she'll have the tenacity to go after what she wants, as you did. Besides, I've already admitted my skepticism was irrational."

"Your words are too big, Daddy," Christy complained in a cranky, sleepy voice.

Jim pulled the small body closer to his side and a few moments of peaceful silence ensued while the child's heavy eyelids closed completely.

A white-winged moth fluttered by, punctuating the darkness that seemed to be closing in on them. Night was falling. Twilight time. It had been a long, long time since Sarah had just sat and watched darkness approach.

"I like this time of evening," Jim said softly. "Too bad we get so busy that we let it come and go unnoticed."

His quiet observation was somewhat unnerving to Sarah, echoing as it did her own thoughts. Looking at him, sitting such a short distance away from her, she was even more unnerved. She wondered idly if she would ever know Jim Laney well enough to tell him about the strange effect he had had on her when she'd first seen him. Then, seeing his subtle change of expression and the sweep of his dark gaze across her face, too akin to a caress, Sarah knew it wasn't necessary to tell him anything. He had shared that moment. The fantasy hadn't been hers alone.

The amber warning light began to flicker, and Sarah decided it was time to channel the conversation back to business.

"I suppose I should ask what you've decided," she said, "since undoubtedly Roger meant for you to evaluate me as well. Now I see why he didn't tell me you'd be here. He didn't want me to be on the defensive. Roger has a very shrewd mind! Perhaps you *should* get him to represent you."

Jim shook his head. "That's definitely out. Roger's convinced me that it wouldn't be good for our friendship. He said that even if we lost and I didn't blame him, he'd feel guilty."

"But you're still not sure about me," she said without rancor.

"In that pretty summer frock, your hair loose across your shoulders, you don't look like my idea of an attorney. In fact if I didn't know better, I'd've sworn you were a model. Sure I had my reservations. However, during the course of the evening, I changed my mind."

"Why?" Sarah asked curiously.

Jim's expression grew thoughtful. "When you choose to, you can be quite haughty. Formidable, even."

"I thought you were married," Sarah confessed with a laugh.

"I figured as much. Anyway . . . I don't know. You impress me, that's all. It would be hard to say exactly why, yet I have the feeling you would be a strong advocate—*or* adversary. Asked to chose, I'd take you as an advocate."

The silence that followed wasn't uncomfortable.

Finally, Jim broke it. "Now it's your turn to tell me your reservations. What were they and why? Do you still have as many?"

Sarah drew in a deep breath. She liked this man. Perhaps she liked him too much. And she was certainly favorably impressed by the rapport he had with his child. Yet she couldn't let personal feelings cloud her professional judgment. Cautiously, she said, "I'll try to work with you on this, Jim. But we don't have to reach a decision right now. Let's discuss the particulars on Monday in my office."

"You won't even give me a clue? Well, I suspect I know some of them."

Sarah started to reply, then looked down at Christy and hesitated. She seemed to be asleep, but Sarah recalled some very interesting conversations she had heard as a child while pretending to be sound asleep. "I'm not trying to be evasive or cagey. I don't, perhaps, agree with everything you've said tonight, but I do appreciate your frankness, and it's only fair and right that we discuss my reservations. But if you don't mind, I'd rather wait till we're alone."

Jim smiled down at his daughter. "I understand. And I appreciate your thoughtfulness. Now, I suppose I'd better get Christy home to bed."

Although neither he nor Sarah said so, they were both curiously reluctant to close the evening. This relationship was a new book to both of them. The next page turned could be filled in varied ways. Or it could be blank. With a wistful look, Jim got up and gathered the sleeping little girl into his arms.

Sarah walked with Jim toward the driveway. When

Jim indicated his car, Sarah opened the door on the passenger side and flipped down the seat. With great tenderness, Jim deposited Christy in the back, making certain she was resting securely before he closed the door.

"Can I give you a lift?" Jim asked.

"Thanks," she replied, "but I brought my car."

"Sticking around for a while?"

"I think not. I'll just look up Roger and Donna and say good night."

"Do me a favor, then, will you? Thank them for me. I hate to go off and leave Christina alone in the car."

"Sure. No problem. See you Monday."

There was nothing left to be said, yet both of them hesitated. Sarah felt a curious desire to touch and be touched, a desire that involved a fine network of emotions including but not entirely based on physical attraction. She wanted to erase the worry lines from his forehead, wanted his fingers to touch her hair with the same infinite tenderness that they had tousled Christy's. Wanting all these things and more, she nonetheless offered a regretful smile as she stepped backward.

As if reading her thoughts, Jim reached out to touch her chin with his fingertip. He inclined his head toward hers, and Sarah noted the strong, masculine sensuality of his mouth. Wanting his kiss, she swayed toward him in a movement barely discernible before she retreated.

"We can't," she stated, the two syllables like blades of grass dancing in the breeze.

"I know." And his hand left her face to fall, palm

down, against her shoulder, where it lingered for a moment at the strap of the sundress, then fell away with heavy reluctance. "For now, we have to keep it business. But after..."

"We'll see," she said softly. With a smile, she said goodbye again and walked away. A part of her was regretful that the fairy tale had to be put on hold. Another part—the part equipped with amber warning lights—was grateful. The magnetism between them was frightening, especially because Sarah prided herself on being level-headed. And, she thought wistfully, the emotional distance required in the client-attorney relationship would give them time to know each other better, to see if this feeling would endure or if it would prove to be as fleeting as a moth's wing against the dark, mid-August sky.

She looked forward to the Monday encounter with Jim Laney and didn't even try to dismiss her nervousness about it as business. Sarah Harbison, the woman, was waiting to see if the mystical quality would still be there. Knowing her life would be simpler if it wasn't, she still wished for it. The usually practical, sensible Sarah was longing for a fairy tale . . . a longing that overpowered even her own warnings to herself.

Jim Laney. When she thought of him, her heart hummed.

All in all, it had been an odd evening. But a promising one . . .

CHAPTER TWO

SARAH DIDN'T HAVE to appear in court on Monday, but her day was heavily scheduled with clients and there was a mountain of paper work. From time to time, she looked up from where she was seated at the expansive walnut desk and smiled to herself. The sparkling clean, plush, and modern offices of Keepers, Donaldson, Payne, and McKinnon bore little resemblance to her grandfather's upstairs office, where she had first fallen in love with the thick, dusty tomes holding so much wisdom and all those mysterious, compelling Latin phrases.

Granddad's office, which smelled of pipe tobacco and spearmint gum, had been crowded with ancient filing cabinets and books and papers scattered helter-skelter. Some things changed with time. Some didn't. One of the things that hadn't changed was the shiver

that went down Sarah's spine when court convened.
As a small child, she had viewed it all with awe. As
a mature woman, she was made very aware of the
awesome responsibility that went with being a good
attorney.

After a light lunch, Sarah asked her secretary to
bring her James Laney's file. She read through the
information with sinking spirits. She had been hoping
she had remembered the facts inaccurately. She hadn't.
As things stood, there simply wasn't much on which
she could base a convincing plea for reversal of custody.

The intercom on Sarah's desk buzzed softly.
Touching the button, she said, "Yes, Leanne."

"Mr. Laney is here for his two o'clock appointment."

"Send him in."

If she had thought his case was hopeless before,
she could have wept when he entered her spacious
office. He wore a naval officer's dress uniform, com-
plete with pilot's wings. *This* hadn't been mentioned
in the material Roger had given her, and it certainly
wasn't going to aid his cause.

"You're in the *navy?*" were her first words.

Smiling at her, a smile even more devastating than
the one she remembered, he said, "I'm fine, Sarah.
Thanks for asking. And, yes, it is a very nice day.
The humidity is way down."

Propping her elbows on the desktop, she rested her
chin on her hands for a moment before looking up at
him. When she did, she had no choice but to return
his smile. "Okay, I admit to being abrupt. You took

me by surprise. I had no idea . . . but anyway, I'm fine too. And the weather *is* much more pleasant. Please have a seat."

Jim sat in the leather chair across from her, holding his officer's cap carefully in his hands. If she had found him attractive in khakis and a polo shirt, he now defied description. Military uniforms with their broad display of bars, stripes, and insignias did much to enhance the appeal of an ordinary-looking man. And Jim Laney was not an ordinary-looking man under any circumstances.

"I didn't mean to startle you," he said. "I just assumed Roger had told you."

"No. And that makes me wonder what other surprises are in store for me. Anyway . . . since I'm not sure where to begin, your, ah, military career will make a good starting place. Do the wings mean you're a pilot?"

"I know where you're leading, Sarah. Yes, I'm in the navy. The wings mean I'm a pilot. The silver oak leaf means I'm a commander. If I had reenlisted, I'd be up for captain next."

"And you aren't reenlisting?"

He shook his head firmly. "No silver eagle in my future. I know a naval career can't be an asset in convincing the court I can provide a stable home for Christy. I was so happy when I got stationed at the base in Great Falls. At last I would be near enough to St. Louis to really spend time with Christy. When I discovered how unhappy she was, I decided it was time to try civilian living. In a few days, I'll have to go back to San Diego. I'll be gone some weeks. But after that, I'll return here with a full honorable discharge. I've already started a business and bought a house in a nice, safe suburban neighborhood. I am serious about winning this case."

"I can see that. Now I hope you won't mind, but I do have to ask you some questions. Some of them might seem personal."

"I expected that. Shoot."

"Your divorce took place three years ago. You made no attempt at that time to gain custody. You didn't even petition for increased visitation rights. Why?"

"I was sent to Guam not long after the baby was born. Joy didn't want to go. She convinced me it wasn't a suitable place for an infant. Possibly, she was right. When I'd been there a year, she filed for divorce. I wasn't surprised, and I didn't contest it. Our marriage had been a mistake. I think we both knew that, even before the honeymoon had ended. Anyway... I was stuck in Guam and Christy was in the States—and such a little baby. I'm trying to be honest, Sarah. Even if I had been in the country, I probably wouldn't have filed for full custody. The traditional way of thinking is that children belong with their mother, especially such small children."

"And what's changed this traditional way of thinking?"

"When I got stationed in Illinois and began to get to know my daughter, I became convinced she was very unhappy. If I didn't think so, I wouldn't be rocking the boat."

"What makes you think she's so unhappy?"

Jim twisted the stiff cap around in his hands and looked at it instead of at her. "She cries when she has to go back. She begs me to let her stay with me."

Sarah had barely opened her mouth when he held up a hand to silence her.

"I've tried to anticipate many of your questions. In the beginning, I thought this was just childish behavior. In broken homes, it's common for a child to play the parents off against each other. And *all* kids put up a fuss occasionally, wanting to stay with their grandparents or someone else. But I know my child well and have observed Joy's actions closely. Christy is lonely. Joy is seldom home. When she is home, she generally has a boyfriend with her, and he'll get most of her attention. On several instances, Christy was left alone in the house. I have documentation to prove this. Joy ignores that child, spends little or no time with her. And she subjects her to verbal abuse— frequently."

"Verbal abuse?" Sarah inquired, arching her brows.

"Whatever you want to call it," he said shortly. "I've observed this myself. 'Don't be such a tiresome little idiot. Go off and don't bother us.' 'Really, Christy, I should think you'd be able to do *something* right.' 'Ugh, get away. You're all sticky. I simply can't understand how *I* had such a messy child.' Except for escorting her to and from the day-care center or to medical appointments, Joy quite literally spends no time with Christy. Children exaggerate. I'm well aware of that, so I checked it out. I've had some very interesting and informative conversations with neighbors, sitters, and teachers at the day-care center."

"And yet this is the woman you chose to marry and make the mother of your child," Sarah pointed out. "Assuming you had a whirlwind courtship and didn't know what Joy was really like until after you had been married for a while..." Yes, assume that, she thought dryly. Wasn't that what had happened in her own marriage?

She watched Jim shift uneasily in the chair. "I suppose, like all of us, my ex-wife has her good points and her bad. I know she isn't a monster. She's a spoiled and selfish woman, very immature. While things are going her way, she can be quite sunny, affectionate, and amusing. You asked about our courtship—well, it was a curiously unromantic affair. Joy Connelly was the daughter of one of my superior officers. I was past thirty at the time and wasn't sure I believed in love as such. From the beginning, I knew what Joy's parents wanted. When she began to push for commitment, I didn't run away. In thinking back, I'm not sure I even proposed. Joy began to talk about marriage; a wedding, I didn't protest. Soon she and her mother were planning ours. That may sound ridiculous, but it's how it happened. Hell, Joy was attractive and had all the social graces and she was certainly used to the military life. I saw her for what she was, but I did think marriage would make her grow up. It didn't. We were both disillusioned and about ready to call it quits, but then we found out she was pregnant. At that point, I cherished the hope that motherhood would have the maturing effect that marriage hadn't. When I had to leave for Guam, things were looking pretty good. Joy was enchanted with the baby and was staying home a lot more."

When he paused for a moment, the story obviously hard for him to tell, Sarah asked gently, "When did her attitude begin to change?"

"I can't say exactly," he replied slowly. "Even after the divorce, Joy would send me pictures of Christina all dressed up in pretty, frilly clothes. She'd write me little notes when Christy walked, or spoke her first words. All that. My leaves seemed few and far apart, and until the past year, Christy was so little that she saw me as a stranger on each visit. But now I see how things are. Joy does dress the child well and have her picture taken a lot. As if she were a doll or some prized possession."

"You don't think Joy shows her any affection at all?"

"I didn't say that. I'm sure Joy loves Christy as much as she's capable of loving anyone. The point is, she's so self-centered that she can't really comprehend another human being's needs. Love sometimes just isn't enough. There also has to be patience, sacrifice—all kinds of things. Christy has nightmares; she wets her bed. Joy simply isn't good for her. I want my child out of that environment before permanent harm is done. Joy. What a curious name for a woman who gives so little to others."

Sarah sighed deeply. The story wasn't so different from others she'd heard. A child couldn't be halved like property or the contents of a bank account. In most cases, one parent got custody, the other visitation rights. She knew it could be heartbreaking to have the amount of time one could spend with one's children dictated by law.

"Neglect is very difficult to prove, Jim."

"I realize that. I hired a detective to follow Joy and log her activities for a thirty day period. I could do it for longer if necessary." Grimacing, he pulled a white envelope from his inside pocket and placed it on Sarah's desk. "You might find this interesting reading. Rather like a tabloid scandal sheet."

Leaving the envelope untouched, Sarah rose from her chair and began to pace the thick carpet. Even in the rather sedate gray jacketed dress accented in yellow and white, her hair pulled into a loose chignon, Sarah knew her effect was a feminine one. There was a softness about her that she knew she had been unable to hide completely behind her businesslike demeanor.

Stopping in front of him, she said with measured forcefulness, and self-assurance, "If a detective followed *you*, Jim, what would the report be like? Do *you* sit home every evening? Have *you* remained celibate since your divorce? No? Then can you give us an estimate as to how many bed partners you may have had?"

"Look . . ." he began.

"No guesses?" she asked archly. "And you dare to cast shadows on the character of your ex-wife? What makes you think you can provide a better home for the child anyway? You've never tackled the task of balancing a job and a family on a full-time basis."

"But Christy is . . ."

Not letting him finish, Sarah went on, *"Surely* you don't pretend you can understand a small girl's wants and needs better than her mother can. And think of uprooting her, of taking her from the home she's always known. Making her the subject and center of a bitter battle between the two people who supposedly love her more than anyone else in the world. It's understandable that you'd like to see your child more. Isn't that the real reason for this suit?"

"I've tried to explain to you . . ."

"Tried. And haven't succeeded, Jim. Are you sure that this whole suit isn't motivated by revenge? Some warped desire to get even with your ex-wife for divorcing you while you were out of the country?"

Her delivery was cold and deliberate. She could tell her words had hit their mark: right between the eyes.

He rose from the chair, his eyes flashing angrily. "I can't believe Roger referred me to you. If you have that little faith in me, then there is no point in continuing this interview. Now, if you'll excuse me . . ."

He turned stiffly on his heel to leave, and Sarah smiled. "Jim," she said softly.

He looked back at her. Noting her smile, he grinned sheepishly, threw his cap onto her desktop, and sank back into the chair. "All right, counselor. You made your point. If you can do that to me, you ought to wreak havoc on the opposition."

"I wasn't really trying to impress you with my ability, Jim. I do know the answers to those questions, well enough to know that your intentions are good. I also have faith that the evidence in that envelope will corroborate your story," she said, pointing to the packet on her desk. "But if you think I was rough, wait till your ex-wife's attorney starts firing the questions. We're going to have to have some satisfactory answers."

"I hope you'll be able to show me the best way to phrase things. As I'm sure you've noticed, I'm not so great at this."

"I'll do the best I can."

"Then you'll take the case?"

"If that's what you want."

"It's what I want," he answered firmly.

Sarah started to pace again, then stopped abruptly and turned to him. "In all fairness, I must warn you, Jim. Your chances aren't good. You have a lot of liabilities. I don't mean that to be a personal insult. But we're going to have to face every angle honestly and objectively if we're going to have any chance at all."

"I understand that. Now, would you mind sitting down while we discuss this? You're making me nervous!" He grinned. "You've already intimidated me thoroughly. Isn't that enough?"

Despite the seriousness of the occasion, Jim's eyes held the mischievous light usually found in the eyes of small boys. Sarah settled back in her swivel chair, cleared her throat, and concentrated on being professional and thorough, despite his charm.

"First, Jim, the fact that you made no attempt to gain custody during the divorce will not be held in your favor. It will very definitely be used against you. Every attempt will be made to distort your reasons, turn them into flimsy excuses. *Then* it was not convenient for you to have her. *Now* it is. Poor Joy is the victim.

"Second," she continued, "you will need substantial evidence that your ex-wife is an unfit parent. The people you talked with will have to be willing to tell their stories at the hearing. Finally, proving Joy unfit isn't enough. You'll have to prove you're better. Much better."

"But I *am* better," he said, grinning lamely.

Sarah chose to ignore this attempt at humor. "As I mentioned previously, no judge will uproot a child unless her present situation is clearly intolerable. Usually, physical or sexual abuse are the only absolute grounds."

He shook his head. "I won't accuse Joy of that."

"I know. And yet other charges are difficult to prove; often they're a matter of opinion. Another factor to consider is that this is the conservative Midwest. While we are making some gains, the instances of the father winning custody—especially over a small female child—are relatively few. Except, of course, when he had custody initially. There is, quite simply, a reluctance in the Missouri courts to revise child custody arrangements. The East Coast and West Coast have been the pace setters in the trend toward allowing a father primary custody. Even then, it's usually granted at the time of the divorce, not as the result of a later suit." Sarah cleared her throat.

"Now, on the issue of your naval career. It's good that you anticipated the problem here. Had you and Joy stayed married, no court would consider removing your child from your home because of a transient lifestyle. But given a choice, a judge would rule in favor of the more stable, conventional way of life. In addition, being a pilot is hazardous, so your decision is doubly wise."

She paused when she saw Jim flinch. She raised her eyebrows slightly, questioning.

Jim answered in flat tones. "My new business is flying, Sarah. We provide courier service, schedule private chartered flights, give flight lessons. I suppose this still comes under the hazardous category as long as I plan to do any of the flying myself."

Sarah turned a pencil over and over in her hands while she listened. This man had so many marks against him that she wondered if it was ethical to give him any encouragement at all. "I'm afraid so," she replied at last. "Piloting would certainly be frowned upon. In addition, this is a new business. Income estimates won't be reliable. You can't prove success, stability, because there hasn't been time. Also new businesses are very demanding. *I* know Christy would come first. That's what this is all about. But a judge who doesn't know either party personally would wonder if you could devote any more time to your child than Joy does at this point."

By now, Jim's eyes held no glint of humor at all. "You paint a grim picture, counselor."

"I know, and I'm sorry. In truth, I've been sitting here wondering if it's ethical to take your case. It will be both expensive and time consuming. I'll do what I can, Jim, if you want to pursue it. Frankly, though, I can't offer you much hope."

"You've spent a lot of time on my liabilities. Don't I have any assets worth mentioning?" he asked, trying to keep his voice light although tension was making itself evident on his features.

"You're honest and sincere. You're so convinced

that your daughter needs you that you've changed your life around completely in an attempt to provide for her best interests. That can't be discounted."

"I can't help noticing it took a lot less time to discuss my assets than it did my liabilities," he said wryly.

"And you still want to proceed?"

"I have no choice," he replied firmly, his eyes meeting hers directly. "My child's emotional well-being is at stake. I'll keep trying if it takes every penny I have. And more, if necessary. Even if I have to beg, borrow, or steal."

Sarah smiled wanly. "Let's try and avoid that if we can."

Jim allowed a crooked smile, but no real gaiety registered. "At times I have the urge just to take Christy and disappear. It would be so much simpler. And faster."

Not entirely sure he didn't mean it, Sarah's reply was quick and rather sharp. "Please don't think that way. There's been a lot of kidnapping lately. Few get away with it. The ones who do it and are located invariably end up the losers when it gets to court. And it's considered very damaging to the child."

"Please," Jim said, holding up his hand. "I have no intention of trying anything like that. I only meant the urge does exist. But long years in the military teach you what to do with ideas like that. Bury them." He smiled.

"Discipline, determination, and strong will?"

"You've got it."

Studying the handsome man across from her, Sarah

mused that it was going to take all the discipline, determination, and strong will she could muster to keep Jim Laney in a comfortable, tidy little niche of her mind labeled CLIENT ONLY: NOT FOR PERSONAL USE.

Jim seemed about to say something when Sarah's intercom buzzed. Reluctantly, she pressed the button.

Leanne's voice announced, "Everett Youngman is here now, Ms. Harbison."

She looked at her watch in surprise. The time allotted to Jim had passed very quickly. With Mr. Youngman, she suspected time would move more slowly. He was an unpleasant man who was squabbling with a neighbor over property lines. As much as she disliked him, she knew he had a solid case. It was ironic, she thought, that Jim, whose motives were so noble would have so little chance, while Youngman would surely win. After all, the neighbor's newly erected fence and storage shed had definitely violated the legal boundary by several inches. Well, justice was blind, she supposed.

"I guess my time's up," Jim said, standing up.

"I'm afraid so."

He hesitated for a moment. "There's so much I feel we still need to discuss, and I'll be leaving for San Diego very soon."

"I can start the proceedings while you're gone," she said gently. "I can do the paper work, request a date for a hearing, feel out some of your witnesses to see if they'll agree to testify."

"I know, but . . . well, I still feel the need to talk about this. If you'll let me take you to dinner, I'm willing to have the time added to my costs here at the firm. It's a rough time for me, Sarah, and everything I've got on the agenda seems so vitally important. There's no way I can get out of this last stint in San Diego. But it means I won't get to see Christy for several weeks, and I'm worried sick about that."

But *I* can't do anything about that, she thought in silent desperation. Jim's love and concern for his daughter were quite evident and, as his attorney, she would do her best to present his case well. However, going to dinner with him and listening to his troubles was not part of her job. She didn't do that for other clients. There was no reason . . .

"Sarah, please."

His dark eyes held an appeal that forced reason from her mind. Obviously he needed to talk to someone. She had no other plans. Why make a big deal over a dinner invitation? As her resistance melted away, she found herself agreeing to a time and place. Although he offered to pick her up, she insisted on meeting him at the restaurant. At least that arrangement made it seem more like a business meeting than a date!

Jim Laney left, and Everett Youngman entered. The remainder of the day was tedious, consisting primarily of paper work.

On the drive home, Sarah found herself wondering what she should wear to dinner. In fact, she gave the matter so much thought that she was practically fuming at her indecisiveness by the time she opened her apartment door. She was too smart—and too honest—to kid herself. It had been a long time since she had fretted about what to wear to a "business meeting" with a client. Serious-minded though she was, she very much wanted Jim Laney to find her as attractive as she found him.

As she put on her makeup, Sarah tried to remember if she had been this concerned with her appearance in the early days of her relationship with Grant. No clear memory emerged and she found that odd, for her memory was usually excellent. Right now, though, she could remember high school dances and dates better than she could her relationship with her ex-husband. Had the bitterness edged out all the good memories? Surely there had been some good times. After all, she had cared for him enough to marry him.

In the mirror, her face seemed almost alien. People try so hard, she thought, to know and analyze other people. And so often, they don't understand themselves.

Maybe, more than she had wanted to admit at the time, she had married Grant because of the security involved. All her friends were getting married. At a certain age it was the accepted thing to do. If so, she had quickly found the security wasn't worth the price exacted. To Grant, a wife was not a person in her own right. She had been his possession . . . an asset chosen to further his political ambitions. His habit of chiding her for her "inappropriate comments" after an evening out, "critiquing" her performance, cut her to the quick. Tears had been to no avail. In his own way, Grant had been a tyrant who would tolerate no opinions other than his own.

Though Sarah felt a certain bitterness toward Grant,

she knew his ran much deeper. In fact, he seemed to hate her. For even when he'd admitted he felt no love for her, he hadn't wanted a divorce. A divorce would interfere with his political ambitions. *Everything* in his life had been centered on those ambitions; she supposed it still was. Why had he been unable to understand that she had ambitions too?

Before things had become totally unbearable, Sarah had suggested starting a family. But Grant had wanted to wait. It would increase his public appeal, he said, if his kids were at the cute and cuddly stage when he ran for federal office.

Now, even when Sarah felt her loneliest, was aware of the void in her life, she was still glad she and Grant had not had children. Children might have kept her trapped in a loveless marriage. Or she could be undergoing an ordeal similar to Jim Laney's. She wondered if Grant would ever forgive her for standing in the way of his political aims. She probably shouldn't care what he thought, but it would be nice to have all her fences mended.

Suddenly, Sarah snapped to attention. Why all this reverie about Grant? she wondered. Perhaps it was her way of registering caution over her strong attraction to Jim Laney. Involvement and commitment hadn't worked for her before. She wasn't quite ready to take that risk again. Maybe she never would be. Being alone could be difficult, yet her marriage had been worse than being alone.

As she approached the entrance of Trader Vic's, her heart fluttered rapidly, another irritating throwback to her adolescent years. As the hostess led her to where Jim sat, Sarah was aware of his appraisal. His eyes followed the sweep of her long, dark hair down to the clingy red dress that was tastefully provocative. She saw he was wearing a white dress uniform, and as he stood up to greet her, she was more pleased than she felt she should be at the idea they made a very striking couple.

After pushing her chair in, he remarked ruefully, "You aren't exactly making this easy for me. Every time I manage to convince myself to see you strictly as my legal counsel, you look so good you're impossible to ignore."

"This dinner was *your* idea," she retorted lightly. "How did you expect me to dress for Trader Vic's? In a dowdy beige housedress? With my hair in a bun?"

His laugh was vibrantly alive. It sent chills down Sarah's spine. "You *are* an amazing woman, Sarah Harbison. One moment you're all sweet fragility, the next all orderly, self-contained competence."

"Does that mean you're still not totally convinced that a woman can be a success as an attorney and still be a success as a woman?"

"Hey," he protested, "I'm not that bad. I'm convinced of your professional ability. Trouble is, I keep wanting to flirt with you."

Smiling, she said, "I rather think you have been. And I suppose it can do no harm, as long as we both know the limits."

"I know them. Unfortunately. But I assume they're only temporary."

And so, she mused, she had what she wanted: Jim's admission that he was very attracted. That it was difficult to ignore. Yet hadn't she known that all along? It was in his eyes when he looked at her, in his voice when he spoke.

Over a delicious dinner of chicken Rea with dry white wine, they discussed the more technical aspects of child custody. And Jim spoke more openly of Joy. A portrait of a very immature, possibly even emotionally disturbed woman grew in Sarah's mind.

"Another thing you'll have to do," Sarah advised, "is provide acceptable answers to questions about your plans for day care and babysitters."

Almost shyly, he replied, "I've looked into all that. There's an excellent nursery school within a mile or so of the house. I have a cousin here in St. Louis. She and her husband are more than willing to help out with Christina when I'm in a pinch. And I'm not trying to separate Joy from the child completely and forever. I want to give her generous visitation rights. I thought I could probably arrange the majority of my out-of-town meetings and whatever for the times when Christy is with her mother."

"You *have* done some thinking."

"This is the most important thing in my life, Sarah."

"Maybe it would help if you married again."

"Forget that," he said, with sudden harshness.

"I was only teasing," she said softly. "Actually, it would be a toss-up as to whether a stepmother would be an asset or a detriment, anyway. If I've learned anything in the past few years, it's not to make assumptions. But you'll have to admit that having a wife to help plan these things—and to help with Christy— would make life easier for you right now."

"Could be. But as I said, I'm gun-shy. How about you, pretty lady? Wouldn't your life be easier with a husband? Perhaps you're gun-shy too."

"Touché, commander. I gather, then, Roger told you I've been married."

"No details," he said hastily. "Just a brief mention that you were divorced. Mind if I ask what this Harbison is like? I can't imagine a man letting you get away."

Not sure she wanted to discuss her private life with Jim, Sarah hesitated for a moment. Of course, she was becoming well acquainted with *his* private life, but that was different. That was business.

"You don't want to talk about it?" His keen gaze pierced through her defenses and seemed to ferret out her most private thoughts.

"I guess not. It's over and done. Only he wasn't a Harbison. He was a Farrell. Maybe you've heard of him. He's making a name for himself in the state senate."

"*Grant* Farrell?"

"The one and only. I took my name back. In fact, I don't think I kept anything of his. And for the record, he didn't exactly 'let me go.' I ran for my life."

"That bad?"

She shrugged diffidently. "For me, it was. For many women, the life he tried to give me would have been a dream. For me, the dream evolved into a nightmare."

Jim looked puzzled at her vagueness, but he didn't ask any questions.

Somehow, she felt compelled to continue. "I guess I have funny ideas, Jim. I really wanted the marriage to work, wanted to give myself to him. But when he tried to change me into something I wasn't, I found I didn't have anything left to give. But enough of that . . . we should leave. The waiter keeps sending us anxious glances. Maybe they need this table."

"Eager to make your getaway, Cinderella?"

"It's been a long, tiring day. That isn't the same as believing my car will turn into a pumpkin," she replied almost defensively.

"I guess that would be a neat trick," he said with a grin. "But really, I don't think you're that concerned that they may need our table. I think you were more concerned by the personal turn of the conversation."

Sarah turned the wineglass around in her hand as she groped for an appropriate retort.

"You find me presumptuous?" he taunted.

"A bit," she admitted. "Or maybe I just find you too perceptive for comfort. When we talk about you, it's business. But when we talk about me, I'm no longer sure of the boundaries."

"Okay," he said cheerfully. "So we'll just keep talking about me. It's a fascinating subject."

Laughing, she said, "I won't debate you on that issue. But I do think we should leave."

With a sigh of regret, Jim got up. As they walked outside, Sarah breathed in the night air. In the daytime it was still very much summer, yet there was a hint of autumn in the night air. It gave her a wistful sort of feeling, a feeling reminiscent of childhood, when this time of year meant a return to school, a loss of leisure time. It was an ambiguous time, a beginning and an end, a change of seasons.

"You're fading out on me," Jim commented.

"Sorry. Just enjoying the freshness of the evening. Feel that touch of autumn, commander?"

"I feel it, counselor."

"The commander and the counselor. Sounds like a Broadway musical."

"Which do you want to write, the words or the music?"

"Both."

"That's greedy," he protested mockingly. "I thought we were going to collaborate."

"You can do the singing and dancing."

"Not unless you want this production to flop," he said.

"That's exactly what I want. A legal tax write-off."

The closer they got to their cars, the more slowly they walked. Underlying the banter was a real reluctance to close the evening. Just when Sarah's warning lights should have been flashing frantically, they were about to dim completely.

"If you'd let me pick you up, we wouldn't have to say good night yet," he pointed out.

"Maybe that's why I insisted. So that saying good night would be easy."

"Only it isn't easy anyway."

Standing by her small blue car, keys in hand, Sarah did not dispute this. "You're leaving for California right away?"

"I'm afraid so. But I may call you once or twice to see how things are going."

"That's fine. Well, Jim, good night. Have a good trip."

"Thanks. Good night, my..." He stopped and

looked at her, a strange expression on his face.

"Is something wrong?"

"No, not really. I found myself ready to say 'my love' without even thinking about it. It was just there on the tip of my tongue, the most natural phrase in the world to use with you."

"Jim..."

Reaching out, he caught a handful of her hair and let the strands drift through his fingers. "Don't keep issuing warnings, my pretty lawyer. I know the rules. But San Diego is over two thousand miles away, and by the time I return, we'll be up to our eyeballs in legal proceedings. One parting kiss can't hurt."

Knowing she should turn away, she didn't. She leaned back against the car and looked up at Jim, making no effort to free her hair from his entwining fingers.

He had a beautiful mouth, although she doubted that he would take that particular adjective as a compliment. Yet is *was* beautiful, both strong and sensitive. It would curve with humor, draw tight with anger, or, as it did now, take on a purely sensual line. She shivered slightly when his hand slipped to the nape of her neck and he drew her face up to meet his. He was probably right... one parting kiss could do no harm.

When his mouth met hers, she was gently accepting. He did not hold her too tightly or make possessive demands. He merely kissed her, but it was with such a great measure of tenderness, it made her eyes sting with unshed tears.

Daring to touch the vulnerable flesh at the back of

his neck, she found it to be warm and firm. Her fingertips grazed the crisp hair, all dark now under the dim streetlights, red hues hidden and subdued. His arms enfolded her completely while her hand that held the car keys dangled at his back and his lips claimed hers again, this time more assertively, yet without loss of the tenderness she needed so badly now. Delicious sensations ebbed and flowed between them. Moonlight made patterns in the darkness. Waves hit against the shoreline. Stars sprinkled against a black velvet sky, one suddenly plummeting to earth.

They stood for a long time, exchanging sweet kisses in the night. It felt so good, Sarah thought, to have someone to lean on, someone to kiss good night, someone to whom to say, "my love."

A shrill wolf whistle from nearby shattered their mood and they pulled away. Feeling suddenly shy and embarrassed, Sarah kept her eyes averted from Jim's. How could she be so inconsistent? How could she be so adamant that they keep things at a business level, then to cling to him with such ardent desperation?

He crooked a finger under her chin and coaxed it upward so that she was forced to look at him. "Miss me, Sarah, my love."

"I shouldn't, but I'm sure I will."

She got into her car quickly and did not watch him walk away. Somehow, right now, she didn't think she could bear to see him leave. All the way home she scolded herself for her idiocy. She asked herself why she had succumbed to him. She had no satisfactory answer.

And, as for the feelings of tenderness, of strength,

of sensuality, that she had experienced . . . well, that was surely make-believe. She wanted Jim to be a tower of strength, a knight in shining armor. Undoubtedly he was just a man. A man like Grant and so many others . . .

When he came back, she would have his case prepared. Professionally, she would do her best, but she resolved firmly to proceed with great caution on the personal level. She'd thought she knew Grant, and had ended up married to a stranger. The way he had tried to use her had hurt deeply enough to leave a scar. She wasn't going to take such a risk again. The next time she let a man have a serious place in her life, she was going to be very sure of him. And she barely knew Jim. Strange, considering that in his arms she had felt like she had come home.

That's what loneliness does to a person, she mused as she drove home, surrounded by silence.

CHAPTER THREE

TIME PASSED SLOWLY, but it did pass. When it came to her work, Sarah kept busy. Her schedule was filled with a variety of cases, which was one thing she valued in working for this firm. Often she had considered how boring it must be to be a lawyer who handled only divorces, only tax cases . . . or only any one thing.

Because her work *was* interesting and appealing, she found herself spending longer hours at the office. In truth, there was little else for her to do. On the few occasions that she accepted dates, she ended up sorry. Involuntarily, she compared each man's appearance, conversation, and good night kiss with those of Jim Laney. Not one of these evenings out came close to approximating the curious though uneasy pleasure she had taken in Jim's company.

They had met only three times, for brief periods, yet his impact on her was undeniable. It was as if his parting words, "Miss me, Sarah, my love," had been a verdict handed down from a judge and jury whose invisibility did not soften the sentence.

She could not escape the feeling that she was behaving like an adolescent. Yet this calm self-analysis didn't succeed in rationalizing away her feelings, either. She told herself the situation was relatively simple and clear-cut: she had been alone a good while now and Jim Laney was an unusually attractive man. That made her easy prey. Because she was, more than she was often willing to admit, a romantic, she was trying to embellish a case of sexual magnetism into more than it really was.

All that was true, she supposed. Yet each time her secretary signaled that she had a call, her first thought was that maybe it was Jim. When it wasn't, her momentary twinge of disappointment was too real to be called by any other name. On the two occasions he did call, the rapid beat of her heart mimicked the rhythms of joy.

She had been in court all Thursday morning and the mountain of mail and paper work waiting on her desk after lunch was depressing. Arguing cases was the exciting part. Reading through stacks of legal briefs was the tedious, less enjoyable part. Although, sighing, she attacked the work with determination, she seemed to be accomplishing little. The papers got shuffled and placed in stacks. The intercom buzzed constantly with interruptions. Time after time, she talked to clients who were concerned over matters so trivial they scarcely seemed to warrant a personal call. Rather crankily, Sarah decided such clients didn't have as much to keep them busy as she did.

Finally, just when there was enough of a lull that she could make some progress, the intercom buzzed again. Sarah gave the instrument a withering look. "Yes, Leanne?" she grumbled finally.

"You have another call, Ms. Harbison."

Waves of irritation washed over her. "Can't you handle it yourself, Leanne? I've already talked to the multitudes today." She instantly regretted her sharpness.

"Uh, it's Mr. Laney long distance from California. Do you want me to take a message?"

Something in her secretary's tone told Sarah Leanne had perceived her eagerness to accept Jim's calls. And without a doubt, Leanne was competent enough to take his message. Probably he had only called to let her know the date of his return to St. Louis and to set up an appointment to discuss the case. She didn't have to talk to him... she wanted to.

"I'm sorry I snapped. I know the interruptions haven't been your fault. Put Mr. Laney on, please."

After a petulant sniff, Leanne pushed the right button and Sarah was connected, via a mass of wires and waves she had never tried to understand, to Jim in San Diego.

"How are you, Jim?"

"Fine. Feeling a bit odd, though. Suddenly I'm a civilian."

"Are you depressed about it?"

"Not really. Just at loose ends. The navy has been

a way of life so long, it seems odd not to be a part of it any longer. Anyway, I'm catching an early morning flight. Since I'm overdue for some time with my daughter, I've already called Joy and made arrangements for that. I'll be picking her up Friday night. From then till Sunday evening, she's mine. How are things going there?"

"Everything is set. The preliminary hearing is scheduled for the first part of November."

"Will you have a few minutes Saturday morning? I'd like to stop by the office and talk to you. I suppose it could wait till next week, but . . ."

"I know you're anxious for the details, Jim," she reassured him, knowing she would make time for him on Saturday morning no matter how full her appointment log might be. "Come by around ten-thirty, if that's all right."

"That's fine. I'll see you then. 'Bye."

With that, he was gone. When the connection was broken, her burst of exhilaration also vanished. Jim hadn't said one personal word. Rationally, it was better that he hadn't. It would have been better, too, had they not exchanged lingering kisses beneath the streetlights of St. Louis, but they had. And now he didn't refer to that episode at all. It was as if he attached no importance to it. As he probably did not, she thought wryly. She had spent nearly six weeks fantasizing like a melancholy fourteen-year-old over something that had not entered his mind again. He hadn't seemed the type, but it was certainly not unlikely that he was a typical sailor, with the proverbial girl in every port.

Although she managed not to snap at her staff and

colleagues, Sarah's foul mood persisted. For weeks she had lived for those phone calls. Now that Jim would be appearing in person, she did an about-face. Suddenly, she didn't want to see him at all—that rat who changed women as casually as he did socks.

On Saturday morning, however, when Leanne informed her Mr. Laney had arrived, her pulse quickened, something that was becoming habitual at the mention of his name, the sound of his voice.

When he walked into the room, magnificent in tweedy blazer and brown slacks, he suddenly seemed to fill it. There was no space his presence didn't seem to touch.

"How have you been, Sarah? You're looking great, as usual."

Somehow, despite her tailored outfit and understated makeup, his dark, desirous eyes told her he spoke the truth. For in his presence, she had felt the change in herself, the subtle alterations no willpower or logic could prevent—a brightening of her eyes, a flush of her cheeks . . .

"You too," she replied honestly. "You're no less imposing in civies, commander, than you were in full dress uniform. Please have a seat."

She hoped that when he was seated across the formidable desk his effect on her would not be so powerful.

"I had to do some quick shuffling through the closet when I got home," he said with an easy laugh. "No one warned me the heat had been turned off in Missouri."

Sarah smiled. "It has been chilly lately. The long

range forecasts promise an early winter. I always look forward to the first frost, when the leaves change. It's my favorite time of year."

"Mine too. Except maybe spring, when everything is green and budding. Or winter, when you can curl up in front of a roaring fire. Or maybe summer, when you don't have to bother with jackets. You can play tennis or swim outdoors any time you want."

Sarah laughed, too keenly aware of everything about him. "So you love them all." As you do with women? she added silently.

"I guess that's what being stationed in California and the tropics so long has done for me. Now I really appreciate the seasons. After a while, all that sameness can be boring."

"I'll remind you of that a few months from now, when we're buried under a few feet of snow."

Weather, she mused. The perennial safe topic. Clearing her throat, she said, "But you're here to discuss your case." In her brisk, businesslike manner, she opened a file marked "Laney" and spread out an assortment of documents and forms.

"What can you tell me about the judge?" he asked.

"He's tough but fair. He's an older man, and that could be a disadvantage. Many older attorneys still hold to the child-belongs-with-its-mother edict, no matter what the evidence. On the other hand, Judge Crawford has always been independently minded. He likes to pull the rug out from under people's feet, so to speak. *That* could be to our advantage."

At Jim's keen look, she flushed and smiled ruefully. "I realize that sounds like double-talk. It probably is. But as we've discussed before, these things simply cannot be predicted. It would be helpful if Christina could testify. However, she's far too young for any judge to request that."

"I don't want her to have to go through that anyway," Jim said quickly.

"I know. Besides, at that age they can't always be believed. They're too easily led and coached. And most kids tend to embroider the truth even without coaxing. But we do have evidence to document your charge that your ex-wife is seldom home. And the fact that you're working so hard to establish a proper environment for Christy shows concern. That can't hurt."

"You want to make an estimate of the odds, counselor?"

"You ask hard questions."

"Admittedly."

"Five to one," she said, after a brief pause.

"I guess it's needless to ask if the odds are for me or against me."

Her voice was subdued when she replied, "I'm doing the best I can. I've spent far more time on this case than on anything else on my schedule. If I hadn't pushed hard, the hearing wouldn't have come till after the first of the year."

"I appreciate that. And doing your best is all that can be asked of anyone. I guess I'd better be going. I brought Christina with me, and she's probably pestering your receptionist to death."

"You could have brought her in."

"I know, but I wanted to be able to talk freely."

"How much does she know about what's going on, Jim?"

"Very little. She's only four, and legal proceedings are confusing to *me*. When she begged me to let her go to San Diego with me, I ended up telling her I was trying to fix it so she could stay with me when I got back. When she was curious about coming here, I told her you were going to help me try to talk Mommy and the judge into letting her stay with me more."

"And?"

He shrugged his broad shoulders. "You know what little kids are like, Sarah. They form their likes and dislikes instantly. Apparently, you impressed her. She thinks you can do anything."

Sarah shook her head. "I wish I could. I really do."

Further exchange was cut short when the door opened and Christina peered timidly into the room. "Are you almost done, Daddy? There's nothing to do out here."

"Come on in, Christy," Sarah said quickly, sensing that Jim was ready to scold the child for her interruption. "We're almost done. And I know there isn't much to do out there but look at magazines and watch Leanne work."

"Daddy said you're going to fix it so I can stay with him," she announced forthrightly.

Sarah shot Jim a murderous look.

He made the correction immediately. "I said she was going to *try*, Christy. That's not the same as a promise."

"I'm working hard on it, Christy," Sarah said. "But try not to be mad at me if it doesn't turn out, okay?"

"Okay. Guess what? Daddy's taking me to the zoo tomorrow. Soon it'll be too cold, and he said we could go one more time."

"That'll be fun."

"Can you come, Sarah?"

"I don't think so, honey. I'm awfully busy."

"But you said it'd be fun. Do you work on Sundays too?"

Two pairs of brown eyes regarded her openly, one pair full of childish curiosity, the other full of amusement at her unexpected predicament.

"I meant it when I said it would be fun," she said carefully, "but I'm sure this is a special day for you and your daddy since he's been gone a while. You'd have more fun without me."

"No we wouldn't," Christy said, seeming puzzled at Sarah's statement.

"I wish you would come, Sarah," Jim told her. "And Christy does too, or she wouldn't have asked."

Suddenly, Sarah felt confused. Wisdom warned her to back off and not become any more involved with these two. Yet she *wanted* to go. Seeing the zoo again after so many years, in the company of an enthusiastic child, would be refreshing. She had become more than a little tired lately of what passed for entertainment in the adult world. And surely she needn't be so leery of Jim's power over her, as long as Christy was along. The little girl would be a shield against his impassioned kisses . . .

"We'll pick you up at one o'clock," Jim said, smiling. "Unless, of course, you insist on meeting us there."

"Pick me up if you like," she replied in a tone considerably cooler than the one she had used in reply to his daughter. She quickly scribbled her address and home telephone number on the back of a business card.

"You surprise me, counselor." He raised his eyebrows at her as he accepted the card.

"The zoo seems safe, commander."

"I wouldn't bet on it," Jim replied, his eyes softening. "And you'll have to stop calling me commander. Now I'm just plain Mister."

Christy scowled at them during the interchange she didn't fully understand. Tugging at Jim's trouser leg, she asked, "Does that mean she's going?"

"It means she's going," Jim said firmly.

After the farewells had been said, Sarah dropped her head to her desk for just a moment. Somehow she always found comfort in pressing her forehead against the polished surface. Back and forth, she thought grimly. One moment she was determined to cut any thought of Jim Laney out of her mind, the next moment she was agreeing to spend an entire afternoon with him. When he was standing before her, looking down at her with those magnetic brown eyes, he had the power to make her resolve evaporate.

Time for such speculation was short. The intercom warned her that her next client was waiting. When free at last from office duties, Sarah went home to attack her shopping and household chores with ferocity. Later that evening she went to dinner and a movie with two old college friends and stayed out later than she had intended.

When she woke up on Sunday morning, she was still quite tired. Her first waking thought was of the trip to the zoo. Glancing at the clock, she toyed with the idea of calling and cancelling out. If it had not been for the memory of Christy's small earnest face, she would have done so. Right now, the child needed a few happy moments, not more disappointments, and she seemed to count on Sarah's presence. If the fact that she cared about disappointing Christy held a warning, Sarah ignored it.

She showered, washed her hair, and blow-dried it. Dressed in a fuzzy robe, she picked without enthusiasm at the light lunch she had prepared.

If, she mused, her heart wanted to maintain a romantic picture of James Laney, perhaps a few hours trudging about under gloomy skies looking at smelly animals imprisoned in cages was what she needed. Maybe at last she would see him as just another human being, not as an intriguing stranger. But what if she found she liked his more mundane side? Well, the commitment was made. She'd just have to take her chances.

Sarah dressed in jeans, topsiders, and a knit wool camisole that had embroidered flowers around the neckline. Over that she pulled on a sweater woven of rich autumn colors, then swept a portion of her hair back on each side, catching it in back with a wide barrette. It was a style she had worn off and on since she was a little girl. Probably it made her look more like a teenager than an attorney-at-law, but she didn't change it.

At the sound of the doorbell, she swallowed hard.

Jim and Christy stood waiting for her, both of them with happy smiles on their faces. As they walked to the car, Sarah was conscious of trying to match her stride to that of Jim's longer legs.

The weeks in California had deepened his tan and heightened the glints of red in his hair. Dressed in jeans and a soft chamois shirt, he looked the picture of health and vitality. Like a model in an orange juice ad, she thought wryly, her cynicism a futile attempt to mask his impact on her.

Cheerily oblivious to Sarah's worries, Christy bounced along between them all full of chatter and giggles.

Observing the child's pleasure in little things, Sarah wistfully felt herself being pulled back in time. She could remember being like that. Once everything in the world had been important and interesting. When had it stopped? When had she become too busy to notice the little things? Or, perhaps, she thought, it wasn't a matter of busyness as much as it was the onset of that much touted state—maturity.

"Chatterbox," Jim teased fondly. "Sarah's going to think I wound you up before I brought you out."

That made Christy giggle and, seated in the car between them, she made a comical pantomine of unwinding. "Do you think I talk too much?" she asked Sarah when she was done with her performance.

"Not at all. Let's just have fun and be chatterboxes if we want to."

When Jim had parked the car, he looked up at the sky, his forehead wrinkled apprehensively. "I was hoping for a nice, crisp sunny day. Now it seems as if we might get rained out."

"It won't rain, Daddy. At least not till after we've seen the monkey show and the elephant show."

"We'll see about that."

For an hour or so, it appeared that Christy's confidence in nature was not misplaced. The sun played a game of hide-and-seek with the clouds. Brightness alternated with gloom. Drawn into the magic of the zoo seen through a child's eyes, Sarah forgot all about her apprehensions of that morning.

The chimps were fun, making faces back at them and splashing water out through the bars, obviously delighting in their ability to make the crowd scatter and squeal. The most beautiful place, Sarah thought, was the bird house with its tropical foliage inhabited by the brightly plumed creatures. Lumbering through the hills created for them, the woolly bears seemed perfectly happy. The only animals that really bothered Sarah were the huge cats who paced back and forth nervously behind bars, seeming to resent their captivity.

Then, just as they had started toward the arena where the monkey show was to be held, the thunder roared, the skies darkened, then immediately broke open.

"Uh-oh," Jim said. "We'd better run for the car."

"But, Daddy, we can't miss the monkey show," Christy wailed.

"If it quits raining, we'll catch the next one. Right now don't argue. Run."

When her small legs couldn't keep up, Jim scooped her into his arms. By the time he reached the car, unlocked it, and deposited the child inside, Sarah caught up with them, panting breathlessly.

All thoroughly soaked, they sat there looking at each other and at the sheets of rain outside. Their sodden clothes and hair dripped onto the plush upholstery. To try to dry everyone out, Jim switched on the heater. They waited for nearly half an hour, but the rain continued relentlessly.

"Christina," Jim said gently, "I think the animal shows will have to wait for another time. It looks like it'll rain all day. Even if it quits soon, the benches and everything else will be all wet."

"But you *said* I could see the shows. You *promised*."

"Hey now, toots. I promised we'd come to the zoo. That's all. The rain's not my fault, you know."

"But I wanted to see the shows, Daddy," Christy whined, lower lip thrust petulantly outward.

"I'm sorry. We'll just have to try again."

"But it's gonna get too cold, you said," she argued, tears beginning to flow freely down her flushed cheeks.

Jim gave Sarah an apologetic grin. "Remember what I said about the frightful fours? You are now seeing a demonstration."

"I don't like you, Daddy," Christy stormed.

"That's enough of that," he said firmly. "Don't talk smart or I won't even try again this year."

The child didn't talk back this time but slipped down into the seat, a small mass of wet dejection.

"Look up, Christy," Sarah said. "Even with all this rain, you can see the arch through the windshield."

"I don't want to see the arch. I see the arch all the time."

"Not like this. Not peeking through the raindrops. See, it's shaped like a rainbow."

Christy looked up rather sullenly. "It doesn't look like a rainbow to me. Rainbows have pretty colors."

"Oh, I think it's a bit like a rainbow. See, it rises from the ground to tower way up over all of St. Louis, then bends down on the other side to touch the ground again. And you can see it from all over the city. It's like the crown of St. Louis. It changes color too. It looks different in sun and rain and each different kind of weather."

Sarah felt Christy's little body relax while she listened. Some of her anger and disappointment was dissipating.

"I guess maybe it's a tiny bit like a rainbow," she conceded. "The crown of St. Louis? That's neat. But *who* was St. Louis? Was he somebody real?"

"I imagine he was, though I don't know anything about him," Sarah admitted. "The French people who came here named the city. In fact, lots of the French tradition is still with us. Like the names of streets and counties."

"Like what?" Christy asked, interested in spite of herself.

"Like Frontenac and Carondelet. Creve Coeur. LaClede and Chouteau."

"Then there's always Chippewa and Grand," Jim interrupted with a teasing grin.

Christy gave him a suspicious look. "Those don't sound the same, Daddy."

"He's making fun of my history lecture, Christy," Sarah said, "but he's outsmarted himself because *grand* in French means 'big' in English."

"I should have known I couldn't score a point in a closed car with two females," Jim said with a mock sigh. Over Christy's auburn head, he caught Sarah's eye and smiled.

It was an innocent enough act, yet it evoked strange sensations in Sarah—a burst of sensual feeling combined with tenderness. As if reading her mind, Jim's eyes darkened and the corners of his mouth quirked invitingly. Safe? Not by a long shot, she thought.

Christy touched Sarah's arm, bringing her back to reality. "Did the French people build the arch before or after they named St. Louis St. Louis?"

"The French didn't build the arch, hon. The city is very old and that arch hasn't been here long at all. The man who designed it was Finnish."

"Finnish? Of course he's finished. You can't have half an arch."

Sarah groaned at the pun, then had the job of explaining it to Christy.

"Do you have to go home yet?" Christy asked suddenly. "We didn't get to stay at the zoo long, but we can do something else, can't we?"

Sarah, attempting to protest, found herself caught up in a gentle web of persuasion that was now becoming quite familiar. Before she knew it, she had committed herself to joining them for dinner.

She hadn't known what to expect of Jim's house; perhaps something a bit barren. Instead, it was an attractive brick home in a nice neighborhood. Still, while the furniture was new and in excellent taste, there were few personal touches in the way of plants, paintings, pillows, and so on. Following her line of gaze over the bare walls and empty tabletops, Jim wrinkled his nose at her. "Looks a bit unfinished, hey? Maybe now that I'm here permanently, I can touch it up a bit."

Christy was eager to show Sarah her room, the one area where finishing touches hadn't been spared. Her furniture was white with antiqued handles and the spread and curtains were pink gingham trimmed with eyelet-edged ruffles. Toys, dolls, and music boxes spilled over into every conceivable space.

Jim offered to fix the steaks and salad if they'd take care of dessert. Christy rummaged around in the cabinet until she came up with mixes for a chocolate cake and icing. Sarah had never had the experience of making a cake with a four-year-old before. It took twice as long with Christy perched on the cabinet while they cracked eggs, stirred, whipped, blended, preheated the oven, and greased and floured the pans. Her pleasure in the accomplishment, however, made the extra time and mess worth the effort.

They ate, cleared the table, and loaded the dishwasher. All the while, the three of them talked and laughed and Sarah and Jim were subjected to a barrage of riddles from Christy. After that, they colored pictures in Christy's coloring books. "Well, what can we do now?" the child asked when they tired of the coloring. Soon they were making up their own story. One would say a few sentences, and then the next person had to take over. The story began with a little girl who trained lions, and ended with a helicoptor landing in the middle of a football field.

The evening grew late. A sleepy, lazy feeling seemed to possess them all. Sarah watched Christy yawn, then stifled a yawn of her own. Glancing over at Jim, she saw he was smiling at her fondly. They hadn't yet turned on the lamps and in the darkening room there were mysterious shadows across his features that only enhanced his attractiveness. The child was there. Nothing untoward could happen. Yet even so, Sarah was keenly aware of the desire in Jim's eyes and of the way his mouth moved slightly, sensuously, as he smiled. He was saying, "I want you" just as clearly as if the words had been spoken.

Flushing under his gaze, guessing that Jim could perceive her own stirrings of need, she turned away from him and let her fingers caress Christy's tangled curls. The hair was baby fine and as soft as silk and a certain tenderness crept in among her other feelings.

Sarah didn't want this day to end. What they had done was really . . . well, really *nothing,* yet she had enjoyed it more than any day in recent memory. They were like a family, the three of them. Sarah noted that since meeting Jim Laney, she had developed a propensity to spin pretty daydreams.

What if this were real? she wondered. What if we truly were a family? It wouldn't end here. I wouldn't have to say goodbye and go back to that too-quiet apartment. I would help Christy with her bath and tuck her into bed. I'd read her a story, hug her warm little body to me and feel her soft arms hug me back, smell her unique soapy sweet smell. Then I would return to Jim. We'd have some quiet conversation, share a light snack or a glass of wine. After that, he'd take me in his arms and we'd go to bed.

Warmth flooded over Sarah as she thought of sharing Jim's bed. Oh, why must he be such an attractive creature? Having been in his arms, having known his kisses, she couldn't help hungering for more. She felt a shameless curiosity about what it would be like with him, beyond the kisses.

As she pursued these errant, wanton thoughts, Sarah could feel the blush rising up her neck and touching her face.

"A penny for your thoughts," Jim said, reaching across the couch to caress her cheek. She met his gaze, ready to make some flip remark that would disguise her feelings, but no words surfaced. He held her eyes with his and thus made love to her without a word, without a touch. A wild and sensual response soared within Sarah. At that moment, she wanted nothing more than to throw caution to the wind and let herself love this man in every way.

"Can we play a game?" Christy asked, finally stirring from her sleepy state.

Jim looked away and the trancelike state was broken. Tension drained from Sarah's body, leaving her limp and confused. Some fairy tale I was spinning, she thought with wry humor. I was about to give it an X-rated ending.

Where had caution gone? Sarah wasn't sure. She only knew that when she was with these two, it was almost as if she became another person. And the real danger lay in the fact that she liked the person she became. She liked being a part of the fairy tale family and rather suspected she'd thoroughly enjoy the X-rated ending, too.

CHAPTER FOUR

"DADDY, I ASKED if we could play a game," Christy insisted.

Jim looked at his watch and cleared his throat nervously. "I'm afraid not, sweetheart. You'd better go get your things rounded up. Mommy will be here to pick you up in just a few minutes."

Christy's little face clouded over and Sarah snapped back to cold reality. This wasn't her child. Christy belonged to another woman. And Jim wasn't her husband, her lover. He was her client. The unseen woman named Joy had been his wife, had lain in his arms, conceived his child. Spinning daydreams about a family that wasn't hers was not healthy.

"Daddy, I don't want to go."

At those words, Sarah's burst of introspection ended. The tone wasn't the same one the child had used when her time at the zoo had been cut short. This tone was petulance; it was desperation.

"I know you don't want to go, bug," Jim said quietly. "We've been having a good time and I hate to see you leave. But you can come back weekend after next."

"*When* will it be fixed so I can stay here?" Christy asked, brown eyes filling with tears.

Jim's face was lined with pain. Sarah looked from the man to the child and ached for them both.

"I can't tell you that. We're trying. Right now, though, you just have to accept things the way they are. Be good now and go gather up your stuff."

Christy stood up obediently and walked toward her room, her back stiff and proud.

"Do you think she'd like me to help her?" Sarah asked Jim.

"She's used to doing it by herself. She might like your company, though. You've sure made a hit with the kid. I already told you that you'd made a big impression on her. Today I think she fell completely in love with you."

And did you? Out loud, she said, "Well, I'll go check on her."

In Christy's pink and white room, Sarah found her placing her clothing in an overnight case. There was an unnatural stoicism in her that sent chills down Sarah's spine. "What about your toothbrush and toys, Christy?" Sarah asked, looking around at the many objects still scattered about the bedroom.

"They stay here," Christy said matter-of-factly. "I have two of lots of things. It's easier."

"I suppose it would be," Sarah said, sitting down on the edge of the bed. "Before you left, I wanted a chance to thank you for inviting me to the zoo today. I almost didn't go, you know. It had been so long, I had forgotten how much fun it could be. Even if we didn't get to stay there long, I had fun."

Christy nodded silently. She wasn't crying. The tears that had threatened to fall in the other room had been held back, but the child's bubbling enthusiasm had also faded. Wistfully, without a trace of a smile, she said, "I'm glad it rained. Almost glad, anyway. I wanted to see the monkey show and the elephant show, but we had a nice time here too. It was fun baking the cake."

"It sure was," Sarah agreed. "Say, there's a lot of that cake left. More than your father needs to eat. Would you like me to wrap some of it up for you to take to your mother? I bet she'd be really proud to know you made it."

"I guess so. It *was* good cake, wasn't it?"

"The very best."

Christy didn't really seem inclined to talk, so Sarah left her alone while she went to the kitchen to place some cake in a container. When she carried it into the front room, Christy was in there with Jim. They were sitting, poised on the edge of the sofa. Christy's overnight case was by the door.

Sarah joined them on the sofa. No one had much to say. The three of them sat, lined up like stick figures . . . and were about as lively. Every time a car passed by, they all tensed. At last, thirty minutes past the designated time, a car was heard and it didn't pass by. The doorbell sounded. Christy walked slowly toward the door without looking back at Jim.

And now I shall face the enemy, thought Sarah. In a few weeks, she would be facing this woman in a court of law and doing her best to prove Joy Laney wasn't providing a suitable home for Christina. Sarah knew, however, that Joy was her foe in another, much deeper, sense. This was the woman Jim had married, had fathered a child by. At one time, he had expected to spend the rest of his life with her.

Joy stepped into the room and her cool blue gaze swept assessingly over Sarah. Although Jim had never described his ex-wife's physical appearance, she was about what Sarah had expected. Joy Laney was a delicately formed blonde who was dressed in tight slacks and a silk blouse with a plunging neckline. Sarah didn't need to see the price tags to know the clothing and the gold bracelets and earrings had cost the earth. Everything about the woman was chic, sophisticated, and expensive.

The expertly styled hair was a silver blond that few women were born with, yet there was no trace of darker roots or of the brittleness that often accompanied constant bleaching. The slender fingers that held the cigarette were carefully manicured and their pale coral color matched the color on her lips perfectly.

Sarah felt a brief stab of insecurity about her own appearance. Although she hadn't looked in a mirror recently, she knew the soaking of earlier that day couldn't have helped it much.

"I see you have company, Jim," Joy said. Her voice was cultured, educated, and brittle.

"Joy, this is Sarah Harbison. She was kind enough to agree to go to the zoo with us today. Sarah, this is Joy, Christy's mother."

The introduction was stiff and Jim appeared quite uncomfortable. Sarah wished she had thought to leave earlier and avoid this meeting. The other woman was sure to realize who Sarah was and Sarah had misgivings about the wisdom of this. Should she let Joy Laney see that it wasn't all strictly business between Sarah and Jim?

"Harbison? Aren't you . . . Ah, yes. Of course you are. Martin has mentioned you to me often. He seems to know you quite well."

"Martin Davis and I have been in the same courtroom on several occasions," Sarah said. She didn't add that it had always been on opposite sides.

Joy laughed sharply. "I don't suppose there are many attorneys who haven't faced Martin in court. He's supposed to be one of the best. At what he charges, he should be. You do know, don't you, Jim, that you'll be paying his bill?"

She turned large blue eyes on her ex-husband with a great deal of hauteur. Sarah looked over at Christy, who was standing by the door. The little girl looked thoroughly miserable, and Sarah took note of the fact that Joy hadn't yet spoken to the child or acknowledged her presence.

"That's only if I lose the case," Jim said evenly.

Again came the brittle laughter. "As I said, you'll be paying his bill. Now, Christy dear, we must run. David's in the car waiting for us."

A scowl altered Christy's small features. "Is *he* coming home with us? I don't like him."

Joy reached over to an ashtray and tapped her cigarette, then rolled her eyes upward in mock desperation. "It isn't required that you like David, Christina. You don't like any of my friends anyway, do you?" Without seeming to expect a reply, she turned back toward Jim. "Tell me, does she resent your friends the way she resents mine?"

"There hasn't been a problem," he replied, keeping his voice calm. "But then, perhaps I don't have as many friends as you do."

Joy smiled widely. She was undeniably a beautiful woman, but there was no warmth to her. "Really, James, don't be modest about your conquests. After all, here you sit with *Ms.* Harbison, all cozy after your little jaunt to the zoo. The *zoo?*" With a lift of her eyebrows and a small, superior smile, she managed to convey her disdain. "How very quaint and domestic," she remarked. "Perhaps I was wrong. You may not have many conquests if you drag your, uh . . . dates to the zoo."

Sarah would have been angry herself if it hadn't been for the dark flush rising up from Jim's shirt collar. Alarm that he might not maintain his control overrode her other feelings. She caught his eye and issued a silent warning.

Shrugging, he said, "I guess I'm just inept, Joy. When I'm ready for pointers on seduction, I'll be sure to ask your advice; I have no doubt you know the score. Now, I believe you said you had a friend waiting. I'll pick Christy up at your place a week from Friday. If you'd rather bring her here, just give me a call."

"Of course. Nice meeting you, *Ms*. Harbison. Undoubtedly we'll meet again."

She walked toward the door, her stride long and sweeping. "What *is* that?" she asked, catching sight of the square plastic container Christy was holding.

"It's chocolate cake," Christy explained. "I made it and I'm taking some home for you to eat. It's really good. Wanna see?" Her small hand moved toward the lid.

Joy shook her carefully coiffed head as if she were in despair. "Don't open that," she said sharply. "You'll drop it and have it all over the place. Actually, Christy, I don't see any point in dragging it home. You know I don't eat cake. And you certainly don't need it. At your age, you can get by with being a little on the chubby side, but you need to watch it. Fat girls aren't much in demand."

"But I *made* the cake, Momma," Christy said defiantly.

Joy looked down at the child with cool amusement. "Did you *make* the cake, Christy, or was it a mix?"

The child looked puzzled. "Well...I...it was a mix, but I put it all together."

"That's not a major accomplishment, Christina. Any idiot can add eggs and water. You can make a cake at home when Debbie's there to help. Now, be a lamb and leave it here. That's a girl."

Christy placed the container on the table, picked up her overnight case, and walked toward the door. Then she turned to face Jim and Sarah. Her brown eyes no longer twinkled. Instead, they were fathomless, deep with the worst kind of pain: acceptance without hope. "Goodbye," she said sedately.

How preferable, Sarah thought, were the sulking and tears of earlier in the day. It wasn't pleasant, perhaps, but such behavior was expected from a four-year-old. It was so much easier to deal with than *this*. She could think of no word that seemed to describe adequately the child's manner.

"Goodbye, Christy. Thanks again for inviting me today." Sarah was aware of a certain unsteadiness in her own voice.

"See you soon, toad," Jim said lightly. "Call me this week if you can work it into your schedule."

Without another word, Christy walked on out toward the waiting car. Joy paused in the doorway long enough to look back at them, arch her eyebrows, and say, "See you in court."

The door closed and soon the sound of a car roaring away was heard. It was terribly still in the room. Sarah couldn't bring herself to look at Jim. "Christy didn't even kiss you goodbye," she whispered.

Jim's voice had a strangled quality when at last he managed to reply. "We've learned not to do that. After ninety-nine bad experiences, we caught on. Now we get in all the hugs, kisses, and 'I love yous' when she comes and while she's here. The affectionate partings always ended up with both of us dissolved in tears and anger."

Sarah knew she should ask to be taken home now. She was far too involved as it was. Still, it seemed that asking to leave right at this moment would almost be an act of desertion. "Want me to make some coffee?" she offered lamely.

"Thanks. Good idea, but let me . . . you're company."

"No, really. That's okay. I want to do it." Alone in the kitchen, Sarah stood by the automatic coffee maker and watched as the dark liquid flowed into the glass pot. She felt quite despondent. Whatever else she had had in mind, fate had intervened. Beyond a shadow of a doubt, she cared for Jim and Christy Laney in a way that went beyond the commitment she felt toward her regular clients. They both touched her in a special way that defied all her attempts to remain distantly neutral.

Carrying the steaming mugs to the other room, she handed one to Jim. For the first time since Christy had gone, she dared to look at him. His face again looked troubled and careworn; he seemed a decade older than the laughing, lighthearted man who had been at the zoo and prepared dinner for them.

"So now you've met the *Joy* of my life," he said bitterly.

Sarah found herself wondering how he could ever have cared enough for a woman like that to marry her. With her, he had been so keenly perceptive, seeming to know her thoughts almost as well as she knew her own. How could he have been drawn to a woman so cold, even callous? But it wasn't a question she could ask.

"From the first time I met you and Christy," Sarah began slowly, "I liked you both. I liked how you were together. I guess that was Roger's motive in bringing us together the way he did. He wanted me to observe the obvious affection that flows between you and your child. You want Christy with you. That's quite obvious, and it's a natural way for a father to feel—even if the child's mother were doing a good job. I don't have kids. But if I did and couldn't be with them . . . I can imagine how hard it would be."

"It's hell," he said flatly, "yet I could accept that emptiness if I knew my child was happy."

"I guess that's what I was getting around to saying. This wasn't exactly the way I would have chosen to meet your ex-wife. Now that I have, though, I can understand how you feel. I never doubted you, of course. It was clear that you were deeply worried, that Christy was anxious. Still, it's a great deal more effective to have a scene like that played out before your very eyes. Everything becomes that much more clear. It's surprising, really. I should think Joy would be on her best behavior, knowing that her custody of Christy is threatened. And it's strange that she grew even more sarcastic and unpleasant once she realized I was your attorney."

Jim's expression was sardonic. "Sarah, Joy *was* on her best behavior. Surely you noticed the way she talked to Christy?"

Sarah was silent.

"That was quite a mild sampling. Small wonder Christy hates it there." Bitterness edged his words.

"I could tell," she replied softly. "Her fear was plain to see. But more horrid than that, I think, was her grim acceptance."

Jim tossed back his head, shutting his eyes tightly as if to fight back tears. "I can't talk about it, Sarah. I know you mean well, but please shut up. I can't take it right now."

The urge to comfort him was overwhelming and Sarah reached out to touch Jim's hand tentatively, almost as if she feared he would reject the gesture and draw away from her. He didn't. Instead, he set down his coffee and covered her hand with his own. Two lonely people, each filled with a measure of pain and confusion. As if with a will of its own, Sarah's left hand, reached out to touch Jim's face. She allowed it to rest gently against his cheek, then trailed a finger along the strong line of his jaw.

When he pulled her into his arms, she went without hesitation. Seated on the couch, her head nestled against his chest, she almost feared to breathe. Close to her ear was his heart, its beat steady and rhythmic. He began to stroke her silken hair, his fingers catching in the fine strands that tangled so easily, restoring them to smoothness. When she removed her face from its resting place and tilted it up toward him, she was silently offering her kiss. He needed comfort and, in her own way, so did she. How long since she had been held and loved? She really couldn't remember. Her last days with Grant had not been affectionate ones. Their physical relationship had become mechanical, something they did almost because it was expected. Making love with Grant had been curiously joyless.

Gently, tenderly, Jim nibbled at her lips, then kissed her closed eyelids, letting his mouth move slowly along her cheek and jaw until it found a resting place in the hollow of her throat. Lingering sweetly, it returned to her lips. "Sarah," he murmured hoarsely. "I need your love."

"Jim, we..." She wasn't sure what she'd been

about to say. Nor did it matter as he kissed her in a new and different way. There was a hungry desperation in the way his mouth ravaged hers. She understood that desperation because he was seeking out pleasure to ease the pain from his soul, at least temporarily. Lips soft and pliant, she matched his kisses with hers. Searching, exploring, yearning, his kisses suffused her with delight.

"You feel so good, my love," he whispered. "Your mouth . . . so hot, so sweet. Please, kiss me that way again."

And she did, glorying in the furnace of his mouth as his probing tongue caused the blood to rush through her veins like licking flames. She wasn't thinking about Grant anymore. There was no time, no room for thought of anything but this moment, this man.

Locking her hands behind his neck, her fingers delighting in the feel of his skin, his hair, she let her tongue move eagerly over his lips, then on to explore his mouth. When she felt his hands move up under her sweater, however, she had the will to pull back. "We can't let this go any further," she said huskily.

He kissed her again, this time quite softly, then looked deeply into her eyes. His were filled with such a mixture of hurt and yearning, she knew that if pressed, she could deny him nothing. From the moment she had seen him in the McKinnons' yard, he had wielded an uncanny power over her. She was strong-willed, yet he always seemed to get what he wanted from her . . . and in a way that made her enjoy the giving.

"What we feel for each other is special, Sarah. What I've seen on your face, I've felt in my heart.

Help me shut out the world. For a little while."

"It isn't wise at all," she whispered, letting her fingers get to know the texture of his thick hair.

"Yes, that's true. Not wise at all."

Seeming to sense her acquiescence, Jim stood up, pulling her close. She rested fully against him, glorying in the return of his demanding mouth, shuddering at the impact his strong, masculine body had on her, reducing every muscle and fiber to quivering jelly.

Arms entwined, they walked toward his bedroom. There, he guided her toward the bed and eased her gently down.

When she started to sit up to remove her clothing, he shook his head. "No, I want to do that."

After removing her shoes and terry crew socks, he bent to kiss each toe lovingly, first the left foot, then the right. Next he unzipped her jeans and slipped them off, dropping kisses on her knees and cupping her silk-clad hips in his hands. Greedily, then, she welcomed the return of his mouth to hers. When he pulled back to kick off his own shoes before joining her on the bed, each second he did not touch her seemed like an eternity. Sarah pushed against him, finding the new sensations exciting and luxuriant. Possibly she had felt like this before. If so, she couldn't remember it. And this wasn't a feeling that would let itself be forgotten easily. She wanted to comfort, to love, to give . . . and she wanted to be comforted, to be loved, and to be able to accept Jim's giving.

While unbuttoning his shirt, she smiled a slow, sweet smile and kissed the crinkles at the corners of his eyes and the sensual corners of his mouth that she so dearly loved.

With a quick, impatient gesture, he shrugged off the shirt, then proceeded to remove her sweater and lace bra. With hands and lips that seemed to know every trick in the book, he searched out the most vulnerable parts of her, leaving a trail of fire in his wake. His movements were slow, lazy, unhurried. His thumbs pushed against her hardened nipples, making them ache with pleasure. When he lowered his mouth to her breast she let out a low groan and pressed his head tightly against her.

By the time he had removed the rest of his clothing and her only remaining garment, she was in an agony with the need to have bare flesh against bare flesh. She kissed his chest, letting the soft hairs that covered it tickle her nose and lips. Their color was a pleasing gold, a slightly lighter reddish brown than the hair on his head. Her hands played along his back and shoulders, feeling the ripple of his muscles.

"You're so lovely," he said softly, letting his mouth feast on her breasts, then move along the flat plane of her stomach.

Again she felt the surge of fire, a fire completely out of control. When he touched the petal-soft skin of her inner thighs, she moaned and called out his name.

"I can't wait much longer, love," he murmured in her ear, his tongue trailing along the lobe.

Sarah drew him down for a long, deep kiss that spoke more eloquently than words. "Then, please, *now*," she said when the kiss had ended.

When he thrust into her, they both cried out in delight at the pure pleasure of being so totally and irrevocably one. Eagerly, she arched against him, hips moving in a timeless rhythm, not wanting to be robbed of one sweet second of his love. In the fierceness of their lovemaking, Sarah forgot all else. Nothing mattered but the fiery joy of this moment. This was a sharing that took them through peaks and valleys of pleasure too intense to be believed. This was the ultimate of all highs, a natural state of being no drug could simulate.

She ran her hands down the entire length of his firm, strong body.

"Sarah," he said. "Oh, sweet. Oh, love..."

His movements became stronger, more demanding. There was an urgency about him that was almost rough, as if he had gone beyond the control necessary to be tender. Moaning, she dug her nails into his flesh and met his urgency with her own, which was just as fierce. She felt needful, wanton. This fevered giving and taking made her feel so very vital. Spasms of delight swept over her again and again, eliciting cries she could not hold back.

"Sarah," he said again, his voice itself a driving force. "My sweet, sweet Sarah."

His words seemed to come to her from a distance, yet she was as close to him as it was possible to be. She said his name also, their voices, their moans, mingling. His claim on her created such an agony of pleasure that she gave herself up to it, now completely mindless with passion. When he gave one last cry and fell against her, she was overcome by peace and the world no longer swayed precariously beneath them.

Sarah buried her face into the hollow between his neck and shoulder and kissed the firm flesh there, its taste salty, sweet, and sexy.

Pulling back slightly, Jim looked into her face and laughed. The pain was gone from his visage. She knew it would come back, yet any respite was welcome. As he had said, they both had a need to shut out the world for a little while.

"Why are you laughing?" she asked, even though she felt the same urge herself. Then, suddenly, the laughter was bubbling to her throat.

"The same reason you are. Because, in the midst of this insane, unhappy mess, we've managed to find each other and a bit of happiness. I love you, Sarah Harbison."

"And I love you. I think I have all along. But I kept telling myself how ridiculous it was, that we didn't really even know each other."

"I know all of you I need to know." With that, he began to kiss her with renewed ardor and Sarah reluctantly withdrew from his embrace.

"You'd better take me home now, Jim."

"I want you to stay with me tonight."

She shook her head and sat up, holding the sheet in front of her. "I can't say I'm sorry this happened. Not right now when I feel so content and fulfilled. But all the same, I know it shouldn't have. Not with your case before us. We said we were going to put the possibility of a personal relationship on hold until after..."

"But you know what they say about the best laid

plans of mice and men," he interrupted with an easy grin that she found incredibly sexy.

"Since you're the man, I gather that places me in the mouse category," she said dryly.

"I wouldn't say that. You weren't exactly mousy tonight," he observed. "More like a tigress."

"Still," she continued stubbornly, "I can't stay. Joy knows I'm here. Just as you hired detectives to watch her, she might have returned the favor. I'm not ashamed of loving you, Jim, but if there's going to be mud slung, Martin Davis will get all the mileage possible out of an illicit relationship between you and your legal adviser. If I spend the night here, it could mean trouble."

He gave a deep sigh. "You're right, of course. I hate to let you out of my sight, but I guess I should just be grateful we had this much time together."

She touched his chin tenderly. "And after the case is over, we'll have the rest of our lives. Hopefully Christy will be a part of that. May I tell you something that could sound silly to you?"

"I want to hear anything you think or feel, Sarah."

"This evening, before Joy came, I found myself daydreaming about the three of us as a family. I enjoyed today so much. Here, with you and Christy, I found something that had been missing in my life."

"Why would that sound silly to me? It's what I feel, too."

"I don't know," she said, shrugging her shoulders slightly. "I guess it's because I've been such a sensible, calm, rational person. It wasn't that I didn't want to believe in fairy tales. I did, but I just never saw much evidence they existed. Ever since you entered my life, I've been hoping for fairy-tale endings."

"I'll give you one," he promised, leaning down to nibble at her neck.

"Don't make promises you can't keep," she said lightly. "We have a long way to go before this is settled."

"Nothing can make a difference in how I feel about you."

Looking deep into his eyes, she felt almost lazy, as though she could drown in them, willingly. She wanted nothing more than to be pulled back into his embrace. Instead, she gathered the sheet about her and began picking up her scattered garments.

"Can I see you tomorrow after work?" he asked eagerly.

Pausing as she dressed, she reached out to place a finger across his lips. "No, Jim, no. We're going to have to go back to putting this on hold until after the hearing. After this evening, it seems futile in a way. I know that, and I'm not trying to pretend that tonight didn't happen. Any objectivity I ever had about the case is gone. You'd better let me try and keep my mind on business."

"Sarah," he said fiercely, "we're going to win her, you and me together. I feel sure of that."

"Jim . . ." she tried to warn.

"Don't start playing the stern advocate." His eyes moved insolently over her half-clad form. "The way you're dressed, the businesslike approach won't work."

She made a face at him. "It would serve you right, Jim Laney, if I never shared your bed again. To *laugh* after we made love. Now that could be seen as an insult."

"Never," he said, his voice warm and affectionate. "To be able to laugh together, before, during, and after love...it's wonderful. Only a perverse mind could take that as an insult."

"Maybe I have a perverse mind. I've certainly changed it enough, lately. Now, are you going to get dressed and drive me home, or are you going to go like that?"

He sighed reluctantly and got out of bed, standing naked before her without a trace of self-consciousness. What a glorious body he had, she observed wistfully, wishing she could spend the night with him.

Later, alone in her apartment, Sarah found sleep elusive. What she had feared most had come to pass. Her life was now inextricably tangled with Jim's...and with his small daughter's.

She was a good attorney. That was a fact she had never doubted. But she was not a miracle worker. With all her heart, she wanted to win this case for these two people, so new in her life and yet so infinitely precious. But her sharp attorney's mind told her this might take a miracle to accomplish.

She had to win. She *had* to. The phrase echoed over and over like a mantra. Or like a prayer.

CHAPTER FIVE

ROGER MCKINNON'S FACE was a study in brooding introspection. The brow beneath his thatch of silver hair furrowed with concern. Impatiently, Sarah shifted from one foot to the other, waiting for his answer. It was evident that he was not pleased with her, but she hadn't expected him to be.

He gave the eraser end of his pencil one final tap on the polished surface of his tidy desk, then spoke with slow deliberation. "I warned you, Sarah. And I warned Jim. But I suppose I'm more to blame than either of you. I should have anticipated that attraction could become a problem in this particular case..."

"Then why were you so insistent that *I* be the one to handle the case, Roger?" Her voice was perhaps sharper than it should have been in addressing her boss.

Apparently perceiving the extent of her emotional

stress, he ignored this. "For reasons I've already out-
lined to both of you, I simply felt you could handle
the job best. It isn't likely that he'll win this custody
case, in any event. Not on the first go-round anyway.
But I felt that if anyone on my staff could pull it off,
you could. I still think so. Even knowing you were
both single and lonely, I told myself there wasn't any
danger of real involvement. You'd both been so badly
burned in first marriages that up till this time, you'd
been extremely wary. How was I to know that after
a few meetings you'd throw caution to the wind and
declare yourself to be in love?"

His remark drew a spark of anger that wasn't easily
contained, but Sarah managed to hold her voice steady.
"You couldn't have known that, Roger. It's the last
thing I expected of myself, but it has happened, and
that's what we have to deal with. I care far too much
for Jim and Christy to want to take the responsibility
for losing. And very conceivably the judge won't grant
custody."

Roger shook his head, and his response was firm.
"No, my dear. You must stay on the case. A change
of counsel at this point would be detrimental. It would
look as if you'd lost faith in him. Jim can't afford
that. And by the way, does he know you've made this
request?"

"No he doesn't. But he would understand my reasons. Please, Roger. Put someone else on the case.
Or better yet, take it over yourself. That's what Jim
wanted in the first place. You know that."

"And as you'll recall, I didn't want our friendship
jeopardized."

"But now I'm in the same position," Sarah burst out.

"Sarah, Sarah," Roger said with a sigh. "It isn't like you to be so overwrought. Please calm down! You say it will hurt your relationship with Jim if you don't win this case. Well, you realize it could be just as damaging if you withdraw from a case and another attorney loses. Don't you see that?"

"I suppose I do. I'm just grasping at straws. Even if Jim didn't blame me, I'd blame myself. But I'll be glad when this is all over with."

"Next week, isn't it?"

She nodded. "And a long, long week it's going to be. Christy is back with Joy. Jim and I have agreed not to see each other except in the office until this is all over with. So we're lonely, keyed-up, and generally miserable. I should hate you for putting me in this position, Roger McKinnon."

"But you don't," he replied with a grin. "Because I'm such a lovable guy. And because you're basically too nice to hate anyone."

"Except myself. And I could well end up doing that. For losing control of my emotions; for getting involved. But since you won't let me off the hook, I guess I should get back to work."

Sarah walked slowly toward the door. Just as she was about to step into the hall, she heard Roger say, "You do know the main reason I selected you for this case, don't you?"

"Because I'm a woman and it will look good in court to have a woman on his side," she answered dryly. "A form of reverse discrimination."

"That was a reason," he agreed, "but not the main one."

"Oh?"

"You're a damn good attorney, Sarah Harbison."

At his words, Sarah blinked back the tears that had suddenly formed in her eyes. She managed to mutter, "Thanks," before she disappeared into the privacy of her own office.

Setting her mind stubbornly to its task, she picked up Jim's file and went through the information once again. Roger was right: she was a damn good attorney. And she had to prove it by winning this case. There was too much at stake for anything less.

When the anticipated court date finally arrived, Sarah was so nervous she couldn't even force down a bit of toast and juice for breakfast. She dressed with care in her conservative navy suit and white blouse, and glancing in the mirror, she hoped her eyes didn't look as haunted and hollow to others as they did to her.

As soon as she entered the crowded courtroom, she knew Jim was there; she was aware, somehow, of his presence. Then she saw him. Walking eagerly in his direction, she registered the warmth in his gaze; it created a glow within her. The smile playing at the corners of his sensuous mouth reminded her of things she shouldn't be thinking about at such a crucial moment. For a second she let herself be Sarah, a woman in love, and a smile crept to her lips as her eyes mirrored the affection so evident in Jim's. Sensing they were being watched, she brought herself back to being Ms. Harbison, attorney-at-law. "It's good to see you, Jim," she said briskly, holding out her hand in businesslike fashion.

Sitting down on their side of the courtroom, Sarah went over with Jim how he should respond to questioning from Joy's attorney. Uneasily, she looked toward the other side. As she did, she met the cool blue gaze of Joy Laney, and caught her breath in surprise.

The young woman seated next to Martin Davis bore little resemblance to the woman she had met at Jim's house. Instead of brittle and sophisticated, Joy now looked feminine and frail. She wore little makeup and her pale hair was brushed into a shining mantle that cascaded around the shoulders of her tastefully demure outfit of winter white. Sarah's heart sank. The hard-bitten image Joy had presented had been a boon to Sarah's hope to swing sympathy in Jim's favor. But there was nothing hard about *this* Joy. She was the picture of sweetness. And if that was how she struck Sarah, who knew better, she realized how Joy could affect Judge Crawford.

A woman as self-possessed as Joy would not, Sarah guessed, be easily confused or upset while on the witness stand. More, her counsel was a veteran divorce lawyer. Sarah had dealt with Martin Davis often enough to know his clients were invariably well briefed and rehearsed. Somehow she felt more sure of her opponent's ability to control Joy than of her own ability to control the volatile Jim Laney, whose emotions were pulled taut. It was understandable that he was on edge about the case, and Sarah knew how easy it would be for a skilled attorney like Davis to irritate Jim deliberately and goad him into an open display of temper or bitterness. And she could imagine how Davis would then twist this to show a personal vendetta against Joy and/or evidence of an unstable temperament in Jim. Either would be to Joy's advantage.

Jim gave Sarah a wry smile when she caught his eye. His eyebrow arched upward as if to say, That's fate.

"You might have warned me she had a softer side," she whispered. "Being prepared does help."

With a shrug he replied, "You were expecting horns and a tail?"

"Of course not, though I wish she had worn them. But I *hadn't* expected her to change from a jet-setter to a choir girl."

"So she fooled you. Once she fooled me. Joy *can* play-act. But underneath, there's a rotten core. We know that." He worked at sounding nonchalant, but there was a brooding, worried look in his dark eyes.

"Let me warn you again, Jim—don't let *anyone* get you angry. Not anyone. I know Davis will try. He's going to say things in such a nasty, insinuating manner that your blood will boil. But what you have to do is smile, show what a nice guy you are, and be calm and in control at all times. Can you manage that?"

"I have to, don't I?" He looked over at Davis. Following his gaze, Sarah found herself more intrigued by Joy than by her lawyer. When she'd first met the woman she'd been puzzled that Jim could marry anyone like that. Now she understood. Jim was an intelligent man, but Joy was a woman who always got what she wanted, and had no scruples about it. She would use every weapon in her well-stocked arsenal.

Her study ended when the judge entered the courtroom and the formalities began. Sarah was summoned to the bench, where she stated the basic reasons for Jim's petition. Martin Davis, in turn, made a brief and rather smug rebuttal, after which the fat, middle-aged judge indicated to Sarah that she could begin calling witnesses. She caught Judge Crawford stifling a yawn, and his obvious weariness made her uneasy. It probably meant he was anxious to get his docket cleared as quickly as possible. It would be far simpler for him to rule that things should remain as they were than it would be to change the previous rulings.

Persuading Jim's witnesses to testify in this suit had not been easy. Although they readily admitted Joy should not be in charge of Christy, they were reluctant to become "involved." Character witnesses for Jim had not been hard to find: his many friends and associates were willing to testify that he was a fine fellow. And his military record and achievements spoke for themselves. But proving that James Laney was a fine fellow really wasn't enough. What had to be established beyond a shadow of a doubt was that Joy Laney was an unfit parent for the small girl.

Under Sarah's careful questioning, a nursery school teacher timidly told the story of a neglected child who was extremely fearful. Several times the judge had to remind her to speak up so that she could be heard more clearly. Her story rang true, yet her timidity bothered Sarah because she doubted that the young woman would bear up under Martin Davis's brand of pressure.

When Davis took his turn at questioning, Sarah held her breath.

"Ms. Cosgrove, you say the child seems 'overly fearful' of her mother," Davis began. "Now, I find that a rather vague statement. Can you honestly say that Christina Laney seems more anxious and dis-turbed than any other child whose parents were recently divorced or separated? Or any child living under other stressful situations?"

"Yes, sir, I can."

Sarah breathed a sigh of relief. Janet Cosgrove might be timid, but she had been persuaded to come here for Christy's sake and it was apparent she wasn't going to back down. She hadn't even qualified her statements with "I think" or "in my opinion."

"Then may I ask," the brash attorney continued, "on what you base such an assessment. Was the child ever marked in any way? Bruised, burned? Did she show any signs whatsoever of physical abuse or make any statements to that effect?"

"Of course not. That isn't what I've said. I said she is a frightened and unhappy child and she is. But I don't think she's been beaten or physically abused."

"Then could you not be taking a very bashful child and blaming the mother unfairly for that shyness? Could you not be labeling simple shyness as fear?"

"No, sir. I've worked with children this age for five years now. I have a master's degree in child psychology as well. Christy Laney isn't a typical shy child. Actually, during the day she relates well to her peers and is quite popular. We give the children tasks and teach them simple things and we've found her quick, bright, and anxious to please. But all of us who work there have noticed—and discussed—that the child does not talk or play in her mother's presence. When it's time to go home, she undergoes a change and grows very quiet and fearful. The other children are glad to see their parents at the end of the day. They're eager to show off their work or relate the day's happenings. Christy isn't like that. She actually dreads going home."

"Come now, Ms. Cosgrove. Aren't you reading more into a four-year-old's actions than you possibly could with any accuracy?"

"More than once Christina has said she wished she could stay at the day care center all the time. I recall telling her that she wouldn't like it there all the time because it was lonely, dark, and quiet when the other children were gone. She replied that it didn't matter because it was lonely, dark, and quiet at home too. It nearly broke my heart. On another occasion she asked one of the teachers if she could come live with her, since the teacher had no children of her own."

Davis smiled indulgently and looked closely at the soft-spoken teacher. "Four-year-old children have big imaginations. They like to talk a lot, don't they, Ms. Cosgrove? I've brought up several children of my own and now have a few grandchildren."

The teacher swallowed hard and seemed on the verge of tears. Yet she gave the attorney a long, level look. "Children are imaginative at this age, Mr. Davis. When they tell me they have green elephants at home or are afraid because there are monsters in the closet, I know what I'm dealing with. When a lower lip trembles every time a child sees her mother and when she remarks wistfully that 'it's lonely, dark, and quiet at home,' then I know what I'm dealing with in that instance also."

Davis then proceeded to question her closely concerning Christy's clothing and personal hygiene. He was trying to paint a portrait of a spoiled, poor little rich girl who was petulant because everything didn't go her way. Janet Cosgrove, however, stuck to her guns. Despite Sarah's fears, the teacher had proved an excellent witness.

Sarah wished they could all have been as good.

One of Joy's neighbors was called. Under Davis's cold gaze and rapid-fire questioning, she dissolved into tears and ended up sounding like a busybody who wasn't really sure of anything, much less that Christy was neglected.

The next neighbor, an older woman, wasn't about to be intimidated by Martin Davis or anyone else. With assurance as brash as his, she refused to be shaken in her story that Christy had come to her home one night quite late, very scared because the babysitter had gotten sick and gone home and her mother wasn't there yet. Apparently the child had been there alone for some time, then began to hear some "funny noises" and ran out crying. The neighbor had returned to the Laney home, put Christy to bed, and stayed in the same room with her, for reassurance. Finally, Joy had returned at about two o'clock in the morning. A male companion was with her, and both seemed "slightly inebriated." The neighbor staunchly maintained that Joy had been quite unconcerned that the teenager had left her child alone and, indeed, was indignant that her neighbor was "interfering."

Sarah's emotions went up and down like a yo-yo. Her spirits rose with the good witnesses and sank with the ones who faltered. She found this as nerve-wracking as her first experience in court—maybe worse. Rarely did she dare to look at Jim. She was afraid that any overt signs of his stress would upset her too badly. Her own tension was extreme. His, then, must be unbearable.

Instead, Sarah turned her gaze to Judge Crawford time and again. It did her little good. Many years on the bench had trained him to keep his expression passive and inscrutable.

After the parade of babysitters and neighbors, Sarah had Jim sworn in. Now there was no way she could avoid looking at him. She fought to view him as just another client when her heart was bursting with love. How badly she wanted to hold him to her and offer comfort! With a calm professionalism she didn't feel, she questioned him about his motives, about the experiences with Christy that had prompted him to request a custody hearing. She was proud of his dignity and bearing. He came across as warm, sincere, and concerned. But, of course, she was prejudiced. Desperately she hoped that he was having the same effect on Crawford.

When Davis took over, Sarah was quaking inside. She was grateful that she was able to sit down because her knees felt too weak and shaky to support her. His approach to Jim was no different from what she had anticipated. Just as she had warned her client, the cross-questioning that had·so annoyed him during his first meeting in her office was mild compared to what Davis thrust at him now.

"It has been frequently mentioned, Mr. Laney, that my client is often seen with male companions whom, your detective notes, have spent the night at her home. A great deal has been made of this. In view of that, I don't feel it would be out of line if I were to make some inquiries about your social life. Have you remained celibate since the time of your divorce, Mr. Laney?"

"No, I have not. Neither have I left my child unattended at the times while she was under my care, nor have I had women spend the night while she was under my roof."

"I see. While it's interesting to have the parameters of your conduct defined, it will be sufficient in the future to simply answer the question."

The malicious questions continued in quick succession yet they were delivered with a smile so benign that one would be hard put to charge Davis with harassment.

By the time he was nearing the end of his questioning, Davis had done his best to make it sound as if Jim Laney were a promiscuous alcoholic who cared less for his child than he did for revenge on an innocent woman who had left him as an act of self-preservation. He also tried to create an image of Jim as a hard-bitten career serviceman, accustomed to a rough and roving life. Undoubtedly he would fail in his attempt to settle down and run a private business—a business that was itself edged in danger and risk.

She had anticipated it all, yet living through it was hell for Sarah. Jim did well, she thought. He answered Davis's questions without evasion and tried to turn the ridiculous insinuations into jokes. From where she sat, Sarah was aware of the veins throbbing angrily at his temples and of the smoldering resentment in his eyes. She was certain that both Crawford and Davis were aware that Jim's attempts at humor were forced and that he was holding himself under control only by great effort. It didn't matter to her what Martin Davis thought, but she sent up a silent prayer that the judge would see Jim as a father under great pressure and not as a tense, ill-humored man.

When Jim was back at her side, Sarah slipped her hand under the table and touched his for just a moment, her fingers exerting a gentle pressure on his before releasing them. Then she returned that hand to join her other one on the tabletop. She and Jim sat circumspectly formal as if they had never touched, never known the pleasures of loving each other completely.

To Sarah's surprise, Martin Davis made no attempt to call witnesses to vouch for his client's moral excellence or maternal leanings. Did that mean there was no one who could so testify? Certainly that could not make a good impression on Judge Crawford. But Sarah knew the ball was still in Martin's corner. Even without character witnesses, Joy, with her demure dress and fair curls, just might be all he needed.

"I . . . I do the best I can," Joy responded to one

of her attorney's questions. Her voice trembled slightly, and she cast beseeching blue eyes toward the judge, "But life is hard for a woman alone. Before I hire a sitter for Christina, I *do* check references and talk to the girls. Most have been very reliable. There were, I admit, a couple of times when we had some misunderstandings."

"Could you explain one of these misunderstandings to us, Mrs. Laney?" Davis's once harsh voice was now a gentle breeze wafting across the courtroom. His manner indicated that Joy Laney was a delicate flower who had to be approached softly and carefully.

"The night Mrs. Anderson described, I had told the babysitter that I would be home by ten-thirty or eleven. When she got sick, she went on home thinking I would be there in just a few minutes and it wouldn't hurt since Christy was already in bed asleep. I never dreamed that she would go off and leave my child like that. Well, we had gotten into this terrible traffic jam and there was no way I could even call. Apparently Christy woke up and panicked. You don't know how terrible it made me feel. And I know I was sharper with my neighbor than I should have been. It *was* kind of her to take care of my daughter until I got home, but she reacted as though I were an irresponsible fool the moment I entered the door. My escort had seen me in, and Mrs. Anderson seemed to assume he was spending the night. She also referred to us as inebriated, but we weren't. We'd had a little wine with dinner, that's all. Her intentions may have been good, but her nose was working too well in more ways than one. And her imagination, too, I might add."

"You do, then, love your child and wish to retain the current custody arrangements, Mrs. Laney?"

She sat on the edge of the big chair, eyes wide with earnestness. "With all my heart. If I lose Christy, well . . . life wouldn't be worth living. She's all I have. From the time she was a tiny baby, it's just been the two of us. Her father was off in Guam. At that time, he didn't seem concerned with Christy's welfare. Or even very interested. She's a bright, well-groomed, well-mannered child. The credit for that doesn't exactly go to Mr. Laney, since he was so conspicuously absent for the first three years of her life."

While Davis led Joy in skillfully portraying herself as a mistreated and misunderstood woman trying very hard to do what was best for her little girl, Sarah restlessly thumbed through the folder. The questions she had rehearsed earlier would no longer work. If she came down hard on this small, pretty woman, then Joy would reap Crawford's sympathy. Really, she thought wryly, the verdict was probably already in. The form of questioning she chose wouldn't matter. Not even when the hard evidence of neglect was before the judge. Joy simply didn't look the part of a neglectful mother. With all her heart, Sarah wished Joy had painted up like a Jezebel, used foul language, and smoked like a chimney throughout the questioning. As it was, she came across as almost as innocent and young as Christina. If Sarah hadn't known better, she might have fallen for the act herself.

"Do you have any questions for this witness, Ms. Harbison?" Judge Crawford inquired.

"Yes, please, a few," Sarah replied, brushing back a strand of dark hair. In her tailored suit with her simple hairstyle, she felt very drab standing before the young woman who was an artful combination of pink, white, and gold.

"I think, Mrs. Laney, we've already established that you spend an average of one night per week at home. What effect do you think your absence has on your child?"

"I guess, Ms. Harbison, to be honest, I hadn't thought about it as much as I should have. My marriage wasn't happy, and it ended on a bitter note. I'm trying to establish a career in interior design as well as maintain a home for Christina. It hasn't been easy. Many of my evenings out relate to business. Even those that might appear social—I have to move around, make contacts. Sometimes, of course, I go out for my own pleasure, to relax. Despite the way it's been portrayed, twisted, I've always taken care to see that the child was provided for."

"Only it often didn't work out that way," Sarah said softly.

To her dismay, tears began to flow down Joy's carefully made up cheeks. "No, that's true. I've made some bad mistakes in judgment, and that was one of the worst. I won't pretend I like it that Jim is putting me through this, but perhaps the experience hasn't been all bad because it has shown me my mistakes. Some good comes out of everything. If I'm allowed to keep my baby—and I *have* to be—than I'll simply have to cut down on the hours I devote to my career and social life. This may cost me a few decorating contracts, but Christy's happiness is my primary concern."

"You thought she would be happy being left with

sitters day and night?" Sarah asked grimly.

Joy sniffled daintily, looking for all the world like a forlorn child. "When I was a child, I was left with babysitters a lot. My father was a naval officer and my mother had to do a lot of entertaining. I never minded. It was just a way of life for us. I knew my parents loved me. Well, I love Christy and I simply didn't realize she was interpreting our life-style as signs of my rejection and neglect. It's shocking and heartbreaking to learn this. Clearly I'll have to remedy things."

Sarah asked a few more questions and received similar replies. She felt like wringing her hands and screaming. This farce had been orchestrated by Davis. She knew him well enough to recognize his hand.

Clearly, Joy had been told not to make excuses, not to seem resentful or be on the defensive. All she had to do was look pretty, dissolve into tears, and say she was sorry, that she hadn't meant to do what she had done. Maybe a different judge would have seen through her; perhaps a female judge. But with a sinking stomach, Sarah knew that Crawford was falling for the act. She had told Jim that he had occasionally been known to grant custody to the male parent. But that didn't seem to be happening now.

When she was done with Joy, the judge called a brief recess after which both attorneys made their closing statements. Sarah's was as eloquent a plea as she had ever uttered. Martin Davis made a brief statement to the effect that his client was obviously not the monster the other side tried to make her seem and that requiring the little girl to change homes at this point could inflict severe emotional injury. He insinuated more than actually stated that Christy's current nervousness was caused by the situation her father had created with his custody suit, and that she had had no problems until Jim resurfaced in her life.

During the break, while the judge looked over his notes in preparation to making his decision, Jim and Sarah walked to a nearby cafeteria for coffee. Across the slick vinyl tabletop, they stared at each other wordlessly. Sarah gazed into the steaming cup of black coffee as if it were a crystal ball that could give her a glimpse into the future.

"We presented solid evidence," Jim said at last. "Davis couldn't bring forth a single person to testify against me. Or for Joy. Surely that can't be ignored."

"Perhaps he didn't need to," she replied, sounding as glum as she felt.

The strain was practically unbearable. They had no words left to express their hopes and fears. The things that sprang to Sarah's mind seemed better left unsaid. It was best simply to wait until they knew the final verdict, she thought. Yet her heart was a lead weight and her body and mind were tired, drained. Call it premonition . . . call it logic. Whatever term were used, she knew she felt defeated.

They walked back toward the judicial building in uncomfortable silence. More than anything Sarah wanted to be able to reach out and touch Jim, to assure him that everything would be all right. Yet something stopped her. Until Judge Crawford spoke, she was Jim Laney's attorney and nothing else. When it was over, she could again be his love and rejoice or weep with him.

As this was only a hearing, the witnesses had gone

home, and the courtroom was bare except for the parties involved and a few people waiting for the next case on the agenda. When Judge Crawford returned from his chambers, Sarah felt numb. His face seemed more lined than it had earlier in the morning and even his black robe drooped.

"Both parties and their counsels may now approach the bench," he said.

The four of them lined up before the judge. Crawford cleared his throat, surveyed the row of expectant faces before him. At last he spoke: "It is the ruling of this court that the child in question, Christina Laney, remain with her mother."

Sarah was aware of Jim's sharp intake of breath. Joy immediately began to bubble over. She tried to thank the judge enthusiastically, but he held up a restraining hand.

"Since Mr. Laney has settled in the area permanently and has established an appropriate home, I feel that visitation rights should be increased in his favor. However, I can see no justifiable cause at this time to remove the child from the environment that has been all she has known. This does not mean, Mrs. Laney," he continued in an admonishing tone, "that this court in any way approves of the evidence that has been presented here. It might be wise for you to think seriously about what has taken place here and amend your life accordingly. Mr. Laney does have the right of appeal, and another court could see things differently."

"Oh I will, Your Honor, I will. I'll do anything to keep my little girl. I want her to be happy."

By the rules of the court they were all compelled

to stand together, one set of people trying to conceal triumph, the other, despair and bitterness, while Judge Crawford went over the revised visitation rights. When it was all over, Sarah walked with Jim toward his car.

"I have another case in an hour or so," she said quietly. "Until then, we can go somewhere and talk."

"About what?" he asked bitterly. He scarcely looked at her.

"Oh, Jim, I'm so sorry. You can't know how..."

"You sure as hell should be sorry," he interrupted, wheeling around to look at her, dark eyes holding no trace of affection or tenderness. "You let that pair of phonies roll over you like steam rollers. It's my understanding that a good lawyer is always prepared for the unexpected. You were about as prepared as Christy would have been. For this I needed an expensive attorney?"

Sarah had expected Jim to be unhappy. But she hadn't expected him to lash out at her personally. He just wasn't like that.

"Jim, I honestly believe I did as much as anyone could have done. I told you from the beginning that your chances weren't good. When I walked in there today and saw Joy, I knew before she even opened her mouth that your chances were diminished. You talk about being prepared. Couldn't you have told me she was capable of such an act? Of the sort of impression she can make?"

"I couldn't have anticipated this. I know that Joy wears many faces, but the woman in that courtroom today was not the one I married. That was an actress, trained to look and act like Rebecca of Sunnybrook

Farm. Joy is an attractive woman. That's true no matter how she presents herself. But she isn't soft, feminine, or helpless. Believe me, I know."

Sarah tried to remain calm. "Even if we had anticipated Joy's plan, we couldn't have done more than we did. Jim, we had *some* evidence. But it wasn't enough. We needed to prove flagrant neglect. In cases like this, the cards are stacked on the side of the mother. I told you that long ago."

"Roger could have flattened them," he said with hostility.

"How do you know that?" she replied, tears stinging her eyelids. "Roger had confidence in me. He felt I could do more for you than he could."

"Then maybe you have him fooled. The same way Joy bewitched Crawford. Roger finds you a very attractive woman. He's made that clear more than once. You are a very attractive woman. A beautiful woman. So is Joy. The weaker sex? Damn, you women rule the world in all that matters."

"Jim," she protested, "I love you and Christy. Don't you know that? Don't you know that gave me the incentive to do my best?"

"Well then, Ms. Harbison, your best simply wasn't good enough. And that little girl is still stuck in that house. Do me a favor and leave me now. I want to be alone."

"Fine," she snapped. "If that's what you want. But when you cool off, think about one thing. This was partly your fault. You wouldn't listen to my advice in the first place. I tried to tell you you were fighting a hopeless battle."

"It meant too much. I couldn't regard it as hope-less."

"I'm a pretty shrewd judge of character, Jim, whether you see it that way or not. I have to be. Joy may have put on a magnificent act today. She seemed much softer than she really is. And to admit to all the charges, tearfully repentant rather than denying, was a tactic we couldn't counter. But she wasn't acting about one thing. She does care for Christy. You try to give the impression she's a total demon. Well, she not. She's spoiled, selfish, and self-centered. I know Christy's hurting because of that, but as you pointed out yourself, Joy doesn't wear horns and a tail. She's a woman with strong points and weak points. Roger told me I was a damn good lawyer. I happen to believe he's right. That doesn't make me a miracle worker."

"I didn't ask for miracles, Sarah. Just competent legal help."

So this is the way it's going to end, she thought dully. She should have known. Their fairy tale beginning had come to a nightmare end. No happily-ever-afters for Sarah Harbison. She didn't even feel she knew the man standing before her. He was as much a stranger to her as Grant had been in the worst moments of their marriage.

"I see. Goodbye, Jim. And if you ever feel the urge to call me again, forget it. I can't think of a thing you could possibly say that could make any difference. Not ever."

She walked away from him and back toward the judicial building as swiftly as her legs could carry her. Urges to cry, scream, and rip things apart raged within her, but she could do none of that. What she had to do was present evidence in her next hearing. During the remainder of the long day, she handled two more cases, both of which were settled in favor of her clients. Sarah Harbison, even when wounded, took pride in her job and did the best she could for her clients. So she had just lost the most important case in her life. That didn't mean she could quit and lose the rest of them.

Dark had fallen by the time she was back in her own office. She sat behind the big desk, not sure what to think or feel and, for the moment, too self-contained to give in to any particular emotion. When she heard a soft knock on the closed door, she wanted to pretend she wasn't there. Instead she sighed and said, "Come on in."

"I heard," Roger McKinnon said simply. "And I'm sorry."

"What did you hear, Roger? That I lost the case or that Jim blames me for it?"

"Both. He came by here and laid a bit of the blame at my feet. I kicked right back at him. In very precise language, I told him what he was acting like. I've never known him to be like this, but surely you can understand the extent of his disappointment and worry. He isn't generally the type to lash out..."

"But for me he made an exception," she said bitterly.

"He'll be sorry, Sarah. Very sorry. I know he cares for you."

"Does he? You wouldn't know it by me. Deliver a message for me, Roger, if the occasion ever arises.

I've had it. I'm not interested in apologies or anything else."

Roger sighed and gave a helpless shrug. "Would you like to come home with me for dinner, kid? I'll give Donna a call. I'm sure she'd be delighted to see you, and right now you sure don't need to be alone."

Sarah made a temple of her hands and looked up at the ceiling. "Roger, I do appreciate your concern. But if you don't mind, exactly what I do need right now is to be left alone. Please?"

"Okay, Sarah. I'm so sorry."

When he was safely out of the room, she let herself go and became only Sarah the woman. The well-trained and disciplined attorney-at-law had forsaken her completely. She wept as she hadn't wept for years, yet the tears seemed to have no healing power. What a fool she had been to let down her guard and allow herself to be vulnerable. Despite all her instincts for caution, she had opened her heart, soul, and body to Jim Laney. Now she was back where she had started, only she was more hurt and confused than ever.

The drive home seemed longer than usual, and as soon as she was inside her apartment, she prepared for bed. It wasn't late, but suddenly Sarah felt very tired.

Maybe Jim was right, she mused sadly. Maybe another lawyer could have won. But what did it matter now? She had lost the case and she had lost Jim and Christy. In time, she supposed, the hurt would ease. But one thing was certain. She would never believe in fairy tales again

What we feel for each other is special, Sarah. What

I've seen on your face, I've felt in my heart. Help me shut out the world. For a little while. The memory of Jim's words sprang unbidden to her mind. Sarah shuddered. All that seemed so far away. Could she have imagined those words? Had they ever really been spoken? Now Jim was somewhere hurt and alone. She was here, hurt and alone. Well, he had made his choice. Let him live with it. She didn't plan to let him—or anyone else—come close enough to hurt her again. Not ever.

CHAPTER SIX

THAT NIGHT WAS the longest of Sarah's life. The next morning she took a look at the pale, wan face in the mirror and grimaced. Then she squared her shoulders with determination and set about the task of getting on with life . . . without Jim Laney. To hide the effects of her sleepless night, she applied more makeup than usual. A thicker layer of foundation covered the dark smudges under her eyes, and peach-hued blusher substituted for the high, natural color that usually stained her cheeks.

She had only been at the office a few minutes when the red sweetheart roses arrived with a sealed card. Sarah removed the card, ripped it in two, and threw it away without reading it. She then took the roses out for Leanne to put on her desk.

Later in the day, Leanne buzzed her on the intercom. "Mr. Laney's on the phone, Ms. Harbison. Shall I connect him?"

"I don't think so, Leanne," she replied, working at keeping her voice cool and controlled. "Just tell him if he wants to discuss the case, you'll connect him to Mr. McKinnon."

The secretary's moment of silence was indicative of her surprise. Sarah could understand that, considering her ill-concealed eagerness to talk to Mr. Laney previously. It wouldn't take Leanne long, Sarah knew, to connect the refusal to talk to him with the rejected flowers on Leanne's own desk. But, truly, she didn't care what Leanne thought about it. Office gossip mattered considerably less than the actual pain she was feeling . . . a pain she was determined to exorcise.

She worked late at the office. When she got home, the telephone was ringing. When it had stopped, Sarah took the receiver off the hook. She thought all the standard things about how she shouldn't do that because, in case of an emergency, someone might need to reach her. But she dismissed such thoughts. She wanted Jim off her mind, and would do whatever it took to achieve that.

The next morning, when the yellow roses came, Sarah took one look at the gigantic fragrant blooms, ripped up the accompanying card, and had the bouquet delivered to the typing pool. For three more days the pattern persisted. Not only did she continue to refuse Jim's calls, notes, and letters, she didn't even acknowledge them.

"When are you going to quit torturing that poor man and let him apologize?" Roger finally asked after the fifth floral arrangement had arrived and had promptly been whisked out of her sight. "It's beginning to look like a damn funeral parlor around here. I didn't know roses came in so many colors and varieties."

Sarah gave him a withering look and replied, "I told Jim after the hearing that there wasn't anything he could say I wanted to hear. And I believe I've told you I wasn't interested in his apologies either."

"Look, kid, I know this is probably none of my business..."

"That's right, Roger."

He continued undaunted. "But I do somehow feel responsible for this whole mess. Jim needs you, Sarah. Now more than ever. Can't you just forgive and forget that outburst of his? He's worried about what he did to you and he's worried abut Christy. After that hearing, he's lower than low. He knows there's no hope for him in an appeal, either. He's seen how effective Joy can be..."

"He wouldn't have won," Sarah said briskly, "even if Joy had acted the jaded sophisticate. Jim simply didn't have a strong enough case. It wasn't as if he hadn't been warned his chances were poor."

"He realizes all that now. Maybe he did all along. He just had a hope, a dream..."

And so did I, she thought bitterly, *so did I.* "Then he won't appeal?" she asked.

"He's not sure yet. He did admit it was hopeless, but he's afraid Christy won't believe he really tried if he doesn't go the limit. I'm trying to talk him out of it. What does a child Christy's age know of appeals

and legalities anyway? I suggested he go to Joy and
approach her in a reasonable way, to see if they can
work out a better arrangement for the child. He says
that's hopeless. I've told him the appeal is, too . . . and
a good way to throw away good time and money. As
you said, we've both told him all along that he didn't
have much of a case."

"And he'll listen to advice now about like he listened then," Sarah stated flatly.

"Don't be so bitter, Sarah love. At least let the guy
talk to you. You aren't being very reasonable."

She shook her head. "Did it ever occur to you,
Roger McKinnon, that even I have a limit to how
reasonable I can be? I will not see or talk to Jim Laney.
Not here. Not at my apartment. Not on the telephone.
So call me unreasonable if you want. I've been called
worse. Once I was married to a man who was sugar
and honey in public and rancid milk at home. It was
an experience that made me cynical about love and
marriage. When I met Jim Laney, I thought I'd found
someone who was different. Well, I was wrong. He's
fine when things are going his way, but when they
aren't, watch out. When Judge Crawford announced
his decision, all I could think of was Jim and Christy.
I wanted to take him in my arms and comfort him.
He showed me very quickly exactly how much he
valued our relationship."

Roger lowered his distinguished head and regarded
her for a long moment. "You've never said a hasty
word and then regretted it?"

"Yes, of course," she answered irritably, "and in
the abstract, I'm willing to forgive and forget Jim's

hasty words. But I'm *not* willing to open myself up to a similar hurt again."

"He's a great guy," Roger said gently. "You don't know that he'll hurt you again."

"And I don't know that he won't. I'm simply not willing to risk it. Since you seem to have made yourself advocate, then you may tell him I wish him all the best."

"And that's the final word?"

"That's it," she said firmly.

With a resigned sigh, Roger went back to his own office.

Sarah's stubbornness persisted a few more days. After that, she was able to think more clearly. She had never been one to place barriers between herself and others who had been important in her life. Grant had resisted her efforts to make their estrangement amicable. Despite what had happened, she really didn't feel comfortable with the way she had dealt with Jim.

If he had been big enough to apologize, she should be big enough to listen—to listen, then to part. She chose to ignore the many times she had woken up in the night, aching with desire after dreaming she had been in his arms again. In time, she assumed, the memory of that shared bliss would fade . . . as would the memory of the later anguish. The fact remained, however, that she had felt more vibrantly alive during that one brief interlude with Jim than she had felt before or since. She had wanted him from the first moment she had seen him. No other man had ever affected her so quickly. And certainly, no one else had had that uncanny ability to weaken her will, make her lose control, to stir her to fiery insensibility. She doubted that she would ever encounter anyone like him again. She shuddered slightly. She hoped not. To feel so much, to care so much, well . . . it wasn't wise. In a relationship, when one person loves more deeply than the other, a state of imbalance exists: too much power on one side, too much vulnerability on the other.

The weekend was cold and dreary. A slow, drizzling rain fell. If the temperature dropped a few more degrees, the streets would become treacherous. Sarah paced her apartment like a caged animal. She knew what she had to do, but a reluctance to take that step persisted. To not see Jim was cowardly. For her sake, and for his, she had to face him, look him in the eye, and say, "It's over, but there are no more hard feelings." Part of her problem was pride. She had always had too much of that. But that was only part of it. The rest, and perhaps the larger portion, was a fear that she would again succumb to his will rather than listen to her own objective reason.

And of course, she thought wryly, she could easily be wrong in assuming he wanted to resume their relationship. He might want what she wanted: to ease his conscience and walk away.

When she dialed Jim's number, her heart was beating wildly. She didn't stop to consider the fact that she still knew it by heart. Everything else about him seemed to be branded into her consciousness. *And this, too, shall pass,* she thought. She had to believe it.

"Hello." His voice hadn't changed. It was still as firm and resonant as ever. But why should she have expected any change? Their time of love had seemed an eternity ago. In reality, it had been less than two weeks since they had parted angrily in front of the judicial building.

"Jim, this is Sarah. Sarah Harbison. I've just been thinking how foolish *and* rude it was of me to refuse to talk to you at all. Roger called me unreasonable. He was right. If you still want to meet with me, I'd like the chance to talk to you."

There was a prolonged silence which could have meant anything. When he did reply, his voice was cautious. "I'd like that, too, Sarah. What did you have in mind?"

The question startled her. She didn't have anything in mind. Just like him, she thought cynically, to put the ball in her court when she had assumed it was his play.

"I don't know," she responded slowly. "Perhaps we could take a walk in the park."

She perceived a measure of amusement in his answer. "A walk in the park? It's awfully cold and rainy for that."

She looked out her window at the grayness and gently falling rain. "Well, I don't suppose it will take long."

"I could come there," he offered.

Sarah looked around at the confines of her small, comfortable apartment. This was her sanctuary, her retreat. The thought of him being here frightened her, suddenly. Was she afraid she would be unable to refuse his kisses? What if he tried to hold her? She did so badly need to be held. Okay, she was strong. She could make it alone. She didn't need a man to love, to lean on. That didn't mean she didn't sometimes want one.

"I'd really like to get out of the apartment for a while, Jim," she fibbed. "If you don't mind, I'd rather meet you in Forest Park. If it's too damp, we can go somewhere for coffee. My treat."

"All right," he agreed. "Thirty minutes?"

"That's fine."

He suggested a section of the park where they could meet. Sarah agreed. They said a polite goodbye and were disconnected. From the moment she had met Jim, opposing feelings had warred within Sarah. It was no different now. Even as she pulled a warm sweater on over her slacks and oxford shirt, then put on her coat, muffler, and gloves, she almost regretted her call.

She had met him in the heat of summer. They had parted in anger in autumn. Now winter was threatening to begin in earnest. Time and love. Both passed and changed. You couldn't hold on to a pleasant season any more than you could to a love grown cold. Those thoughts were with Sarah as she eased her small car into a parking place near where they had agreed to meet. Within moments, she saw Jim's car turn the corner. As she walked toward him, she could feel the light rain against her hair. It was quite cold out and she was glad she had worn the heavy brown woolen coat and plain muffler. He looked so utterly fantastic that she couldn't find words at first. Without the sun's rays beaming down on him so fiercely, his hair seemed darker. His suede jacket was a becoming shade of rust. Whatever her feelings for this man, she could not deny his overwhelming attractiveness. His overpowering masculine presence wasn't something that could be ignored.

"You're looking good, Jim," she said, knowing the casual comment was a profound understatement.

"And so are you. I like your hair that way, falling loose and free on your coat collar."

Sarah reached up self-consciously to touch a strand of the dampening hair, then shrugged. "I really didn't do anything with it. I just brushed it and let it have its way."

"Then it knew what it was doing," he said softly, his eyes boring into hers, evoking thoughts and memories she had been trying for two weeks to lay to rest. "You still want to walk in this?"

"If you don't mind," she said with a small laugh. "Just for a few minutes. Then, if you'd like, I'll buy the coffee I promised you."

They walked through the desolate park. A mixture of light rain and heavy fog enveloped them. Involuntarily, they seemed to try to match their strides. Yet the awkwardness persisted. What had once come so naturally was now difficult to reproduce.

"I'm really sorry," she said at last. "I shouldn't have refused to talk to you all that time. It was childish of me."

"I hurt you," he admitted freely. "I don't blame you at all. God knows why I lashed out at you the way I did. Or maybe He knows. *I* certainly don't. I would rather cut my own heart out than hurt you, yet I ended up doing exactly that. I'm sorry."

"It doesn't matter," she said quickly. "We all get angry and say things we shouldn't."

"Sarah, is there any..."

"How's Christy?" she interrupted. "I've thought of her often."

The broad shoulders inside the suede jacket fell. "Things are much the same. She was disappointed. Very disappointed, but we had a long talk and she seemed to understand. I've tried to tell myself I was overreacting. Maybe I exaggerated her unhappiness because I wanted Christy with me—and she seemed to want that too. Maybe I'm overdramatizing when I worry that she's being harmed psychologically. She isn't beaten or starved. She has enough pretty clothes and toys for several little girls. So why am I worried? Lots of kids live through deaths, divorces, and broken homes."

In spite of her determination to be politely detached, Sarah felt the tears stinging her eyelids. That precious little girl deserved a loving atmosphere. Her own grief and outrage were considerable—and quite apart from her feelings for Jim.

"Talk about it if it helps," she said. "If not, you don't have to explain. Maybe you lack proof for a court of law. What we both have is perception, intuition, a plain old gut feeling that something isn't right in that home."

"I feel so helpless."

"So do I."

He turned to her for a moment, his dark eyes roving

over her face. "Have you had enough of walking in this miserable weather? I'm ready for that coffee you promised me."

"All right," Sarah agreed. "I don't regret my suggestion, though. Nothing like fresh air to clear the mind."

"Or to make you appreciate getting back inside again," he muttered.

They avoided each other's eyes as they entered the small café and hung up their damp coats. But seated across a table in a corner booth, eye contact was inevitable. Jim looked at her in much the way he had before. His expression held a mixture of tenderness and desire which Sarah found it hard to deal with.

He sipped from the steaming cup and seemed hesitant to speak. "You didn't read any of my notes and cards, did you? That's the impression I got from Roger."

She shook her head slowly and looked down into the dark liquid instead of at Jim. "I was too angry, too hurt."

"In them, I asked you to come back to me, Sarah, to give me a chance to show you how much I love you. That's what I still want."

There was long silence during which they both drank the hot coffee. Sarah turned the cup in her hands, grateful for the warmth it provided.

"It's over for you, isn't it?" he asked, supplying his own answer.

She knew she must choose her words carefully. "I don't hold anything against you, Jim. But I'm not ready for commitment, love, marriage . . . whatever it is you have in mind."

"Once you thought you were," he reminded her gently.

"This gets confusing. It's going to be hard to explain without making you think I'm still angry. That really isn't the issue at all. When you asked about my marriage to Grant Farrell back in Trader Vic's, you teased me about my reticence in talking about it. Well, you were right. That experience left a lot of scars. I'm not sure about anything anymore, really."

She paused while the waitress refilled their cups, then went on. "I wasn't just a kid when I met Grant. I had already passed the bar exam. Professionally, I knew who I was and what I wanted. But I wasn't very experienced about men. When I was younger, I was so studious and serious-minded, so fiercely ambitious, that I suppose I frightened off guys my own age. Grant is a good deal older than I am. He was—*is,* I suppose—attractive, and when he wanted something, he had enough charm to get it. I was impressed by him. And I was certainly flattered by his attention. *Everybody* adores Grant Farrell. Men seem to respect him. Teenage girls hang posters of him in their rooms. Toddlers let him cuddle and kiss them without protest. Elderly people think he's just terrific. In fact . . ."

Her tone was becoming increasingly agitated and Jim watched her, raising an eyebrow in faint surprise. "Well," he interrupted gently, "the man does put forth a good and forceful image. You telling me he's a phony?"

Sarah took a deep breath, then blew it out slowly. "I honestly don't know. I do know he has enormous ambition. His ultimate goal is to run for president of the United States. It wouldn't surprise me if he made it." She sighed.

"The trouble with our marriage," she resumed, "arose early on. It happened...well, because I am who I am. Grant cannot tolerate disagreement from anyone who is close to him. Before we were married, he reacted to my 'radical' opinions with amused indulgence. After we were married, his reaction was quite different. He had outbursts of anger during which he said terrible things. He threw things, called me names. He never actually struck me, though there were times when he came close. I was quite afraid of him, actually."

"That sounds pretty bad," Jim said grimly.

Sarah met his eyes. "Yes, I suppose it was. After a while, we seemed to fight over everything—whether I had talked too animatedly to a man at some social function. Flirtatious behavior wasn't becoming to the wife of a public figure. Then, of course, we differed on just about every political, social, and moral issue. You name it. Grant couldn't tolerate that. Anyone who disagreed with him was considered 'stupid,' and my failure to comply also meant I didn't bear him the respect he deserved. The rebellious wife." Sarah looked at Jim uneasily, wondering if she were revealing too much. But the sympathy in his expression encouraged her to go on.

"But the major issue was my dedication to my career. I devoted time to that that he felt should be devoted to serving as his hostess. There didn't seem to be any room for compromise."

Jim lit a cigarette and drew deeply on it. Sarah glanced at him quizzically. He smiled. "I'm still trying to quit," he said sheepishly. "I now only smoke at stressful moments. You know, Sarah, I certainly don't doubt your word. But it's very hard to reconcile what you're telling me with the man I read about in the papers, hear interviewed on TV. He seems so . . . well, almost appallingly reasonable and calm."

"Yes, I know. Well, now you know the other side. Leaving wasn't easy, Jim. I don't take marriage lightly, and I don't like failing at anything. Grant, of course, was devastated. How would this affect his political plans? It wasn't a matter of love any longer. That was long since gone. But he made it very difficult for me. He didn't want me to leave, and he made sure I suffered for it."

A shudder ran through her slender body at the thought of her divorce, how miserable all that had been. Jim reached across the table to touch her hand. She hadn't wanted him to touch her, yet she was glad he did. A bit of comfort, a bit of warmth, a bit of friendship. That was all, she told herself firmly.

"Sarah Harbison," Jim said softly, "that's an awful story. And if it's any comfort to you, Grant Farrell just lost my vote. For all time." He smiled at her in a way that coaxed an answering grin, despite the heaviness of the moment.

"However," Jim continued, "I don't really see what that has to do with us. With you and me. I went through a bad marriage too. Until I met you, I wasn't sure it was even possible for me to love a woman. But I know you're in no way like Joy . . ."

"How can you know that?" she interrupted. "I'm an ambitious lawyer. I have no intention of giving that up. Maybe I wouldn't have any more to give a husband and a child than Joy does. For the most part, I blame Grant for the failure of my marriage, and I say he wanted everything his way. Yet I did refuse to give up my career. I suppose I still feel guilty about that."

Jim retained his hold on her hand as he put out his cigarette. "You're nothing like Joy, Sarah. Sure, you're ambitious. You're also warm, affectionate, and considerate. And surely you can't be implying that I'm like Grant? I mean, I know I blew up at you, but . . ."

Sarah flushed slightly and withdrew her hand, picking up her coffee cup again. "I suppose that's what I thought at first. I wasn't being very logical. It was a gut reaction. Now that some time has passed, I can see the situation more clearly. I can see that I was expecting you to be Prince Charming. I thought we had a fairy-tale romance. No room for ugliness. But that's ridiculous. We're both just people, with all our faults. As I said, it's difficult to explain. I certainly don't think you're as twisted as Grant Farrell was . . ."

"Gee, thanks," Jim said, making a wry face.

"Please. You know what I mean."

"I'm not so sure."

"You hurt me very much. While I'm not holding that against you, my own reaction to that hurt disturbs me. I simply am not ready to run the risk of getting that deeply involved again."

"You're going to hide from life?"

Feeling terribly unhappy and uncomfortable, Sarah

shifted in her chair. "Put it that way if you like. But I have way too many doubts to believe I have anything to offer anyone at this point."

"Are you saying you don't want to see me anymore?"

Sarah looked across the table. Looking into his dark eyes, she couldn't say that at all. "I . . ." she faltered. "Jim, I don't want to lose track of you completely. I'd like for us to be friends. And I'd like to see Christy from time to time. After all, we got along well and she needs a friend too. But as for . . . as for . . ."

Not being able to say the words, she blushed hotly and had to lower her eyes.

"You don't want to sleep with me again," he finished.

That wasn't how she would have put it. And it certainly wasn't how her body felt. Seated across from him, feeling his knee bump hers occasionally, watching his strongly attractive face, remembering how good it had been between them . . . well, she couldn't deny her very human needs and reactions. The point was, she didn't intend to let those feelings rule her life as they once had.

"It's best we don't, Jim. At this point, I honestly think we both need moral support and friendship a lot more than we need entanglements. We're neither of us really ready for that. We tried to tell ourselves we were because the physical attraction was so strong. And if I had ever learned to be casual about such things, I suppose it still wouldn't be a problem, but the fact remains . . ."

"For goodness sake, don't go apologizing for that.

Believe me, I don't care for the decision you seem to have reached. Neither do I want you to be casual about such things. That's what made that time we had together so precious, so special. Because it wasn't casual, it wasn't cheap. It was loving, sharing, caring. That can't be wrong."

"I didn't say it was wrong," she said quickly. "I just said I don't think we're really ready for it."

"Speak for yourself," he retorted, subjecting her to a purely sensual appraisal that made her toes curl with desire.

"Jim," she protested, laughing despite herself.

"Okay," he said, sighing reluctantly. "I'll be good. Friends, huh?"

She lowered her head slightly, then offered her hand.

He took it and raised it to his mouth, dropping a brief kiss on her knuckles. Then he squeezed it tightly before releasing it.

The waitress came and offered more coffee. They both refused. Sarah tried to remember how many cups they'd downed, and couldn't.

"Well, counselor, I'm not sure where this leaves us."

"You will be my friend?" she said.

"I'll be your friend," he promised. "And I'll never ask you to do anything you don't want to do. Fair enough?"

"Fair enough."

They walked back to where their cars were parked. The temperature had fallen and moisture had frozen across the windshields.

"I'll call you sometime and we'll do something. As friends, of course. Are you any good at poker?"

"I don't know," she said with a smile. "I've never played."

"And I don't suppose you're wild about squash or handball either. Tell me, what do you do with your *friends?*"

"Usually we go shopping and talk about men and clothes."

"Jolly. That sounds like loads of fun. Maybe we should meet at some lingerie store downtown."

Sarah laughed, watching her breath make clouds in the cold air. Jim was quite a man. His brown eyes still clearly registered his unhappiness, yet he was able to joke around. Perhaps she was being a fool. While she was playing her game of caution, some woman might snatch him away.

But she knew she couldn't think that way. To lose him now would be better than losing him when they were more involved. It was better than giving herself completely only to find that he wasn't what he appeared. She wanted to trust him. With every fiber of her being, she wanted to trust him. But the experience with Grant had made trust so very hard. What people were on the surface, what they were beneath. One couldn't really know.

"Do keep in touch," she said lightly, sliding into her car. She busied herself trying to find the defrost knob. When she looked up, Jim had already pulled away.

She felt a curious sense of loss. Maybe even disappointment. What had she expected? That Jim would sweep her into his arms and refuse to let her go? That he would react in some dominating, forceful way and override all her objections? But wasn't that just what she'd told him she didn't want? Ah well, she was just too confused.

It was several days before she heard from Jim again. Even then, it was quite by accident. He had stopped by the office to pick up Roger for their Wednesday afternoon racquetball game, and Sarah ran into them in the hallway.

"It's good to see you, Sarah," Jim said politely. He looked so good it made her heart pound. "We still haven't set up that appointment to go lingerie shopping," he added with a grin.

Roger gave Sarah a mildly curious look.

"Inside joke," Sarah explained.

A few days later, Jim called her at home. After a rather stiff greeting, he said, "Upon serious consideration, I've decided against lingerie shopping. How do you feel about poker? Strictly penny ante, of course. I wouldn't dare suggest anything illegal."

She pretended to give his suggestion serious consideration. "I wouldn't mind trying my hand," she said finally. "As long as we don't have to play in a cigar-filled room."

"Pity," he retorted mockingly. "That's an integral part of the game. Well then, how about a tour of my new business?"

"That would be great," she replied with genuine enthusiasm.

"Then that's an acceptable activity for friends to engage in together?"

"Quite acceptable," she returned, unable to keep the happiness out of her tone.

On the appointed day, Sarah was more than a little nervous. As they drove to Jim's new office, the conversation didn't seem to flow. But once there, she found the tour fascinating. There was a large hangar, where the company's three planes were kept. Back in the large, modern office, he showed her an impressive array of charts, explaining both the courier and charter services in some detail. At last he introduced her to his staff. Jim's subordinates were all respectful and friendly, though he didn't go into lengthy explanations of what Sarah was doing there.

"Want to take a ride someday?" he offered when they returned to the hangar. He was bracing his hand against a Cessna that he had called a small plane but that looked large to her. "I took Christy up last weekend. She loved it."

"I'll bet she did," Sarah said, mentally conjuring up a picture of the auburn-haired little girl in the plane piloted by her daddy. "I'd love to. How's Christy doing, Jim?"

He turned slightly and made himself very busy adjusting a knob by the hangar door. "Okay, I guess. She seems a bit listless to me. Maybe it's just my imagination."

"What about the appeal?"

"I've filed. I thought Roger had told you."

"No. Roger doesn't mention you unless I do."

"Anyway, he thinks I'm crazy. Probably, I am. And it certainly isn't as if I have money to burn. And honestly, Sarah, I don't expect to win. It's just as I told you once a long time ago. I want to be able to look at Christina and tell her I did everything I could."

Sarah wasn't certain what she had expected out of this friendship arrangement. Yet when Jim took her home, she felt a certain disappointment. He told her he had to be out of town a good deal during the next few days and would call when he returned.

After a week or so, he did. The invitation apparently was a spur of the moment thing. Jim and Christy were going to go eat pizza and see a movie—would Sarah like to come? Sarah was terribly pleased to see the child again and touched at the warmth of her welcoming hug and kiss. Jim maintained a low-key manner. He made jokes and light conversation, but Sarah could sense a distinct remoteness. It was as though his mind wasn't really on what he was doing.

It was nearly three weeks before she heard from him again. This time he was making good his offer to take her up in one of the planes. Sarah thoroughly enjoyed the short flight over St. Louis. They bobbed and weaved through the clouds and picked out familiar sights in the city below. Jim made a few teasing attempts to scare her with dips and other fancy maneuvers, but Sarah wasn't really frightened. She could see that he was an excellent pilot, and in his hands she felt safe.

The flight came to an end when Jim's secretary radioed up that there was a problem. One of the pilots had called in sick and Jim would have to find a substitute to fly to Cincinnati. Jim told Sarah he had a feeling who that substitute would be. On the way back to the landing strip, her eyes focused on his strong profile. He never seemed to really look at her. Not once, she reflected, in all the time they had spent together. Not that it mattered, of course, she told herself sternly. Casual friendship had been her own suggestion.

"I'll run you home first," he said.

"No, really, that's okay. I know you're needed here. I'll just call a taxi."

"That's a lousy way to treat a friend . . . drive her all the way out here, then make her go home in a cab. Look, take my car, Sarah. I insist. One of the guys here can give me a ride when I get back. I have an extra set of keys, so don't worry about it. Just lock it and park it near your place. I'll pick it up later."

"Jim, really . . ."

"I insist," he said, planting the keys firmly in her right hand. "See you later."

For a brief moment their eyes met and held. Sarah thought, for just a moment, she could see all the old emotions: hurt, love, desire. But with a flicker of long, dark lashes, those emotions were veiled and Sarah could not fathom Jim's thoughts. He seemed so very remote. How safe for her. How sane, sensible, and safe. And how very dull.

All the way home, Sarah told herself she was an idiot. And there was no one to disagree with that assessment.

CHAPTER SEVEN

THREE LONG DAYS and nights later Jim's car remained where Sarah had parked it. It served, somehow, as an irritant to her as she came and went. She was beginning to wish she had left well enough alone and not tried to ease hard feelings between them. With anyone else, the new terms of the relationship might be possible and workable. With Jim Laney, she had her doubts.

She wanted him. She didn't want him. She yearned for him to touch her. She feared it. She didn't like being around him because it was so awkward. She couldn't stand the suspense and loneliness when she didn't hear from him. All in all, it was the most torturous situation she had ever found herself in.

"Go home, Sarah."

Sarah looked up from her desk to find Roger

137

McKinnon regarding her reproachfully. She was surprised to see him there. She had thought she was alone, and Roger didn't make a habit of entering her office without knocking.

Glancing at the clock on the wall, she looked at him curiously. "It isn't late at all."

"True. But it's snowing like crazy out there. Everyone's getting out of here while the getting's good. Forgive me, but I even took the liberty of telling Leanne to go. She was riding in a car pool with some others and . . ."

"Sure," Sarah replied. "Well, then, I suppose I'll follow the crowd."

She began to stack papers neatly and prepare her office for the night.

"Want me to take you home?" Roger asked. "You can leave your car here. It'll be safe enough."

"Thanks. That's all right. It isn't that far to my apartment."

Roger walked with her to the parking garage.

"I understand you still see Jim from time to time."

"Occasionally," she replied in an off-hand manner. "Nothing heavy. Just friends."

"I'd place a heavy bet on whose idea *that* was," he quipped.

"Does it matter?" Looking up at him, she grimaced wryly, then laughed. "Actually, Jim's car has been parked at my place for over three days now. It's a good thing we're living in liberated times *and* a big city. Otherwise my reputation would be in shreds."

"There are worse things than shredded reputations."

"Oh? Something tells me a lecture is on the agenda."

"From me?" Roger asked innocently. "Never. But that doesn't mean I think it's good to exist in a vacuum. Someone smarter than I am said, 'No man is an island,' Sarah."

"I'm not a man," she replied lightly.

"I've noticed that."

"Oh yes," she teased. "I understand you told Jim I had the body of Venus and the face of a madonna. Until then, I hadn't thought you'd noticed."

Roger laughed, though his color deepened several shades. "I'm happily married, my dear. That doesn't mean I'm blind. Are you still determined to keep my friend shut out?"

"We reached an agreement," Sarah said warily. "And that's between *us*, Roger. Neither one of us is ready for anything deep."

There were a few moments of companionable silence. When Sarah reached her parking spot, she took out her keys. Instead of simply saying good night, Roger cast a pensive look at her. "Love is a lot like war and death, Sarah."

"How's that, boss?"

"It's just something that comes whether you're ready for it or not."

She unlocked the car and slid behind the steering wheel, then shot him an impish glance. "You make love sound pretty gruesome, Roger. Thanks for caring, but there's nothing you can do to change how I feel."

"I guess not. Did anyone ever tell you you're too darned stubborn? It's a good thing you *are* so pretty. No man would put up with you otherwise. Drive carefully."

"You too. Good night."

By the time Sarah reached her apartment, the snow was several inches deep. If it kept snowing like this all night, there'd be no way she'd make it to the office in the morning.

Sarah changed from her navy suit into faded jeans and an old plaid flannel shirt several sizes too large for her. She had just snuggled into a comfortable chair with a novel when the doorbell rang.

Opening it, she found Jim Laney standing in the hallway, snow still glistening on his hair and coat. "I finally made it back to get my car," he said with a grin. "Bet you thought I'd abandoned it."

"I hadn't worried," she said, smiling. "After another day or two, I was going to auction it off to the highest bidder. You picked a perfect day to come for it."

"The way things are now, Sarah, I don't pick times . . . they pick me. I wouldn't have made it today except that I have to pick up Christina. I just got back in and found a message from Joy that she had left Christy with a sitter. Joy had to make an unexpected business trip. I can have Christy for a few extra days if I want her. *If* I want her. Joy. If I live to be hundred, I'll never understand . . ."

"Why not come in," Sarah offered. "Don't just stand there in the doorway."

"That's all right. I've got to hurry. Want to come with me?"

Sarah looked about at the empty apartment. "I'd better not. If the weather isn't too bad, I'll have to go to work tomorrow . . ."

Jim stepped into the room and closed the door behind him. For a moment, he was very close. Too close. When he looked down into Sarah's face, she felt as though she were drowning.

"I'll make a deal with you. You come with me to pick up Christy and spend the evening with us. Bring your things along for tomorrow. I'll see you get to work if I have to hire a snow plow. How's that?"

"Is this a ploy to get me to spend the night?" she asked, only half teasing.

"You doubt my integrity? Have I bothered you lately?"

The answer to that was an unqualified no. It was not a comforting thought, somehow. "Sorry," she said lightly. "Anyway, I suppose Christy will be an excellent chaperone."

"Hurry then. Grab what you need."

Within ten minutes Sarah had everything she could possibly need all packed up and ready to go.

"Got snow boots?" Jim asked when she walked back into the front room.

"Snow boots? No. Will I need them?"

"Better bring them. If I get off in a ditch, you'll have to push me out or go for help."

"Now I know why you invited me."

"Never could fool you for long, could I?"

Sarah went back to the bedroom and returned with her knee-high fur-lined boots and a stocking cap. Jim grinned at her as he picked up her bag, then waited as she turned down the thermostat and checked the lights and locks.

Outside, the sky was completely gray. The snow

was already several inches deeper than it had been when Sarah had arrived home. Some part of her willed it to snow on and on—to strand her at Jim's house with him and Christy. But she pushed such thoughts aside.

When they reached Joy's house, Christy came out to meet the car, a wide smile on her face. Jim ran toward her, picked her up, and swung her around and around. "Am I going with you *now*, Daddy? It isn't Friday yet."

"That's quite all right. You're going with me. Run get your things. Hurry fast as you can because it's snowing hard and we need to get home."

"Debbie's here."

"I'll take Debbie home."

Jim walked back to the car and opened the door on Sarah's side. "Come on in and help her get what she needs for a few days. I'll explain to the baby-sitter."

The child greeted Sarah with almost as much enthusiasm as she had Jim. When everything was settled and locked up, they climbed in the car. Christy insisted on sitting on Sarah's lap. By the time they reached Jim's house, it was quite dark and the snow-fall had reached near-blizzard proportions. Sarah envisioned an evening curled up by the fireplace watching TV or playing kiddie games with Christy. Popcorn after dinner, she thought.

She hadn't counted on the way an enthusiastic four-year-old and her indulgent father would view the year's first sizable snowfall. After a quick meal of hot dogs and french fries, Sarah found herself being bundled

up and pulled into the backyard. Jim rigged up a
floodlight at the back of the house, and soon they
were busy constructing a snowman and an igloo.

"I don't think I ever built a snowman at night before," she remarked.

"But the snow might be *gone* by morning," Christy
pointed out.

Sarah looked down at snow up to her knees and
laughed. "I don't think there's any danger there."

"Aren't you having fun?" the child asked.

"Of course."

"Then let's see that she has more fun, Christy,"
Jim said, grabbing Sarah by the coat to stuff a handful
of snow down her collar.

Laughing, Sarah retaliated by catching him off guard
a few moments later. Bent over and unaware, Jim
could do little to defend himself when she pushed him
against the icy igloo, giving his face a good washing.
The three of them laughed and played until they were
so cold their teeth chattered.

"We'd better go in," Jim remarked. "It's late, and
we're all about to freeze."

"But, Daddy, we haven't made snow angels yet,"
the little girl protested.

"Well, by all means, let's do that. Where shall we
do it?"

Christy picked out a place in the yard where no
one had yet walked. In the pure, unsullied snow, she
threw herself down and spread out her arms until she'd
left a wing-shaped imprint. Then she stood up. "Who
goes next?"

With a good-natured grin, Jim fell down and made

his angel, then looked at Sarah pointedly. Shrugging, she lay down in the deep snow and made her imprint next to his. At Christy's insistence, Sarah wrote their names above their imprints.

"Look at that," Christy said with childish satisfaction. "It's a snow-angel family. Daddy Angel, Momma Angel, and Little Girl Angel."

Sarah felt Jim's eyes on her. Not really wanting to look at him, she nonetheless felt compelled to do. Had it been smart of her to come here? No. Was she sorry? Not really.

"Can we take a picture of the snowman and snow angels, Daddy?"

Jim seemed unable to move his gaze from Sarah's face. Finally he answered the child. "My camera doesn't work well in the dark, hon. We can take pictures of the snowman and igloo in the morning."

"And the angels?"

Sarah looked up at the sky. "Snow's still coming down, Christy. The angels will be all filled in by morning."

"Then we'll just have to make more."

"We'll see. Right now I'm only interested in getting inside and warming up."

All three of them made a big production of stomping snow from their boots and shaking it from their coats. Nevertheless, the kitchen was filled with puddles of melted snow by the time they were unbundled.

"I'll throw some more logs on the fire," Jim offered, "if you two will fix the popcorn and hot chocolate."

Curled up before the roaring fire, toasty warm and

comfortable, Sarah confessed that this was how she'd anticipated spending the entire evening.

"No spirit of adventure," Jim replied with a shake of his head.

With Christy present, it was easier than usual to talk. But the vigorous romp in the snow had taken its toll and the child soon gave up her attempts to hide the yawns that were becoming more and more frequent. Sarah felt touched, almost awed, when Christy shyly requested that she help her get ready for bed. As she helped the little girl into the warm dropseat pajamas and turned down the bed in the pink and white room, she couldn't help but remembering her fantasy of long ago . . . long ago, when she and Jim had made love. Reality was coming very close, she mused.

Christy scampered off to kiss her father good night, then returned to her room. Sarah sat on the bed next to her and began to read her a story from a worn copy of Grimm's fairy tales. After only a few pages, Christy was sound asleep. Sarah pulled up the covers and kissed her lightly on her soft, warm cheek. What a lovely child, she thought. If only . . .

But she was determined not to think that way. She couldn't allow herself to become vulnerable again.

She walked slowly back to the room, where Jim had stretched out in front of the fireplace. He was reading from a book that looked more informative than entertaining. The topic was aerodynamics, she ascertained from the cover.

He glanced up and smiled but didn't move. "Would you like some wine or something else to eat?"

"No, thank you. I'm fine."

"There are plenty of books and magazines around. Just find something you like, Or, turn the TV on, if you like. It won't bother me."

With that, he lowered his dark head over the book. Sarah picked up the evening paper and stretched out on the couch. She read everything she found interesting and a few things she didn't. By the time she had made a thorough perusal of the *Post Dispatch,* Jim was still reading intently from the textbook.

No, she thought wryly, this evening wouldn't be like the last one she'd spent here. Jim seemed to be determined to ignore her.

She began to nod. When she stretched lazily and yawned, Jim looked up at her. His brown eyes flickered with emotion. But then he seemed to draw a mask over his face.

"The spare room is the one next to Christy's. The bathroom is across from it."

"Thanks. I believe I will turn in. But let me clear up this stuff first."

"That's all right," he said quickly. "You're tired. Go on to bed. I'll do it. It'll only take me a second. Good night, Sarah."

"Good night."

She was halfway down the hall, almost out of sight, when she heard him call her name. Heart racing, she looked back at him. "Yes?" she breathed.

"If you really have to go to work tomorrow, there's an alarm clock on the bedside table. And don't worry about waking me up. I'm an early riser anyway."

"Thanks," she said, her heart sinking. Slowly, she made her way to the bedroom, feeling like a fool.

Here she was in a war with herself over whether she should give in to him or not, and he wasn't even trying!

She slipped into her flannel nightgown and settled down under the covers. As she tried to sleep, images of Jim lying before the blazing blue and orange flames of the fire danced before her closed eyes. Such a romantic setting! Yet he had kept his eyes glued to a text on aerodynamics. She wondered if she had done her job too well. Had she turned him off completely?

When she stumbled out of bed the next morning at the sound of the alarm, she found Jim and Christy preparing breakfast. For so early in the day, they were disgustingly cheerful. Sarah looked out bleakly at the white snowdrifts. Her prediction had been accurate: no trace of the snow angel family remained. But a quick call to the city offices told her the courts would still be holding sessions.

Now that Christy was present, Jim was his old, talkative self. They kept up a stream of nonsense all the way to the offices of Keepers, Donaldson, Payne, and McKinnon.

It had taken them more than twice as long to get there than it would have in good weather conditions. When Jim pulled into the parking garage, he offered Sarah a wry smile. "You really think you'll be busy enough today to justify getting out in this? Such dedication."

Sarah looked around at the nearly deserted parking garage. She wasn't about to admit it to Jim, but she was beginning to wonder the same thing. "There's always work to be done here, Jim. Even if they cancel court hearings during the day, which I doubt."

"Very well. Want me to pick you up tonight?"

"Oh, that's okay," she said quickly. "I have no idea when I'll be leaving. So much depends on who manages to make it to the courtroom this afternoon. I'll catch a ride with someone or get a taxi. Thanks for the evening. You too, Christy. It was fun."

"Will you come again tonight? We have to make our snow angel family over again," Christy said eagerly.

"I don't think so, hon. But I'll see you again one of these days."

"Soon?"

"Probably. Goodbye, Christina Laney. Be good."

"I will. 'Bye, Sarah."

Sarah closed the door and started walking across the nearly empty parking garage. When she had gone only a few steps, she heard Christina's voice again and looked back. The little girl had rolled down the car window and was leaning out smiling broadly. "I love you, Sarah," she called.

Sarah felt a lump rise in her throat as tears welled up in her eyes. "I love you too, Christy," she managed to reply.

And it was true. She did love the child with an affection quite apart from what she felt for Jim. That was part of the problem. If upon so short an acquaintance she felt this urge to make Christy happy, then what must Jim feel?

Suddenly, Sarah had a bitter thought. What if Jim had only used her? He had expected her to help him regain custody of his child. Had he really cared for her as a woman? Or had he seen her primarily as a help-mate in his dealings with Christy? Sarah had fought his custody battle for him—however unsuccessfully. And she could form a ready-made family for him now, providing warmth and that motherly touch during visits from his daughter. She doubted any such motives could have been conscious on Jim's part. He wasn't a demon. Yet her whole relationship with him, professional and otherwise, had been predicated on the child. Mightn't his feelings have become confused? Perhaps that was why he was able to stay up long into the night, calmly poring over aviation books. While Sarah lay in bed burning for his touch . . .

She pushed these thoughts away.

But soon they were replaced by others. Walking into the cold, dark office she turned on the lights and mused that it was very possible—even probable— that Jim still harbored some resentment against her because of the defeat in the hearing. Sure, he had apologized. But ever since they had spoken that day in Forest Park, he had been so unbearably cool, so contained, so reserved. Again she told herself that it was she who had asked him to keep the relationship on a less personal plane. Yet if he loved her, wanted her, could he possibly hide it so well?

Very few people had made it into the offices by midmorning. Sarah made coffee and had a cup in solitude. Gradually, a few hardy souls dribbled in, but the offices seemed hollow, empty. When the word came to her that all court appearances for the day had indeed been postponed, Sarah felt defeated. Why had she insisted on coming in? What would the day have held if she had stayed with Jim and Christy? Sarah closed her eyes. They would undoubtedly have had a lovely time. But wasn't that precisely the problem? Oh, she was so confused!

Sarah turned to her paper work, but having put in such long hours recently, she didn't have much left to do, so her thoughts about the Laneys persisted unimpeded. Making a sudden decision, she scanned her calendar and schedule of upcoming cases, then walked toward Roger McKinnon's office. If anyone else would make it to work despite all obstacles, it would be Roger.

She was right. Dressed casually in corduroys and a sweater rather than in his customary suit and tie, Roger sat behind his desk.

"May I talk to you, Roger?"

"Sure. Come on in,"

"I've been under a lot of stress lately, and I was wondering if you'd object if I took a week of my vacation time now. My schedule is pretty light right now, but in a few weeks that should change. So, if you wouldn't mind..."

He looked up at her, his eyes filled with amusement. "I've been waiting for you to take a break," he kidded. "By all means, please! Go! Are you going anywhere in particular?"

Tossing back her hair, Sarah grinned at him. "I really don't know yet. I hadn't even thought about it."

"Look, Sarah, you haven't taken my advice so far, so I should give up trying but..."

"But you're not about to," she finished, smiling fondly.

"That's true. All I was going to say was that I don't think it would be good for you to mope around that apartment for a week. Take a cruise. Go somewhere. And don't tell me you can't afford it. You can afford to go someplace nice."

"I'll think about it."

"Don't just think about it. Do it."

Actually, Sarah had intended all along to go away. She wasn't running away, she was merely putting some space between herself and the two Laneys.

Back in her own office, now that her impulse had become reality, Sarah felt the first stirrings of real excitement and anticipation. She picked several travel bureaus out of the yellow pages and called them to compare prices and arrangements. Within an hour, she found herself booked on a flight to Jamaica for the next day. The weather there, she was told, was gorgeous.

She called and arranged for transportation home, then stopped by to give Roger the name of the hotel where she would be staying. "For emergencies only," she said.

"Fine," he agreed.

Back at her apartment, Sarah's excitement grew as she hunted around for shorts, sundresses, and bathing suits. She was going where there wasn't a snowflake within miles, and she was going to lie around and be lazy and get suntanned!

She wore her heavy woolen coat over a light-weight traveling ensemble to the airport. In a few hours, she was getting off the plane with the coat tucked under her arm. She smiled happily, breathing in the salty sea air. She was very glad she had come.

*   *   *

Sarah spent two days on the beach doing little but soaking up the sun. Evenings, she circulated among the other tourists and got well enough acquainted with a few to have some dinner companions. And she loved Kingston. It was a lovely tropical city and it offered much in the way of sightseeing. In fact, Sarah was so intrigued by it that she only thought about Jim Laney eighty percent of her waking moments instead of the usual ninety.

The third day, she went to her favorite spot on the beach. Stretching out the beach towel on the sand, she removed her white terry-cloth coverup and lay down with a sigh of contentment. Even in Jamaica, where scantily clad bodies were the norm, heads turned as Sarah walked by. Usually she would not be aware of this, but now was flattered. It must be the new red bikini, she thought. But it was more than that, she knew. For the first time in a long while she was beginning to relax, and it showed.

Sarah read for a while, then swam, then read some more until the sun made her sleepy and she felt consciousness begin to drift away.

"Pardon me, but is this spot taken?"

At the sound of the familiar voice, Sarah's eyes flew open instantly. Startled, she sat up and stared into Jim's eyes in disbelief.

"Jim?"

"I think so. Last time I checked my driver's license, that's what it said." The corners of his eyes crinkled as he looked down at her. He was wearing dark trunks and had a towel slung over his arm. Calmly, he proceeded to spread out his towel and ease his large frame down on it. "I would tell you how beautiful you look, but with what I'm thinking, I might end up getting slapped. Even arrested."

Sarah laughed. "I would ask how you knew I was here, but I suspect I already know."

"Roger didn't want to tell. I had to threaten him with physical violence. But anyway, I happened to have a flight scheduled down this way . . ."

"You mean you flew?"

"Sure," he said breezily.

"But why, Jim? Why did you look me up?"

Jim rolled over on his side, propped himself up on one elbow, and looked directly into her eyes in a way that made her heart turn over. "I don't really want to talk right now, Sarah. Do you?"

Sarah's heart pounded as she struggled to meet his gaze. When it came to Jim Laney, she had never had a chance. "No," she whispered.

They didn't look at each other as they stood up, picked up their towels, and dusted off the sand. Jim didn't touch her as they walked across the beach, into the hotel, and across its spacious lobby. Knowing he was behind her, conscious of every breath he drew, Sarah led the way to her room and unlocked the door. As soon as they were inside the room and the door was closed behind them, she felt herself pulled into his arms, pressed against his firm, warm body.

Being held by him was a homecoming. It was Christmas. It was the Fourth of July. It was wonderful. She knew she had missed him, but she hadn't known how much until she was pressed tightly against his chest hearing him whisper her name over and over. Their lips met, gently at first, then with deepening passion.

"We really should talk about this," she murmured, kissing the corners of his mouth and taking playful bites of his upper lip. Moving back, she placed her hands on his shoulders and looked deeply into his eyes.

He laughed. The warm, throaty sound made her pulse leap. "Talk, talk, talk. And when silence is so much nicer." Shifting position, he stood behind her to circle her waist with his arms. He pulled her back against him until she could feel the full length of him. Suddenly she wanted to sink, to lose thoughts of all else but his very real and very physical presence. Sarah tossed back her head until it rested on his bare shoulder and he bent to kiss her neck with a slow, sensual yearning that added fuel to the desire already raging inside her. She wanted to turn in his arms and feel the full glory of his kisses. But she stayed as she was, savoring the tenderness of his kisses on her temple, on her eyelid, across the sweep of soft hair.

"I've missed you so," she whispered.

"Tell me about it," he said softly. "Tell me about sleepless nights and endless days and phones that don't ring. Tell me."

His hands moved from her waist up to her breasts, cupping them, feeling the taut nipples with his fingertips. He let go of her then, and his fingers undid the fastener of her red top. As it fell to the carpeted floor, Sarah turned and pressed herself against him, then gave him her open mouth to explore with his own hot and eager one. Need ebbed and flowed between them, a very tangible need that throbbed and ached for fulfillment.

"Sarah, love me," he said huskily, and Sarah knew she would. Now, forever. She shivered and leaned back, supported entirely by his hands clasped tightly at her waist. She could feel the burgeoning evidence of his need of her. The fever raged and, stepping away, Sarah stumbled. Her own need was so great that her body could hardly support itself and even her vision seemed blurred.

Meeting his eyes, she slipped out of the bottom of her swimsuit.

"You're so beautiful," he said huskily. "I don't think I'll ever be able to look at you enough."

"You don't plan just to look?"

"No," he whispered. Letting her go briefly, he stepped out of his trunks and stood before her without shame.

The sight of him made Sarah's own aching more intense. She held out her arms and he came to her, holding her for a long moment. Then they moved toward the bed, tumbling onto it, their limbs entangling delightfully.

Sarah ran her hands across his chest, trembling at the sensations that touching him evoked. He kissed her breasts and fondled her hips and thighs until she thought she would go out of her mind with pleasure.

"Sarah, love me," he whispered again. Gasping, Sarah parted her legs, shuddering as he buried himself deep within her. Later could come the exquisite moments of teasing and gentle torture. Right now the need was too immediate to be delayed, a driving need that must be slaked. It had been so long, so very long. She closed her eyes and arched against him, moving, swaying, giving and taking with that magical, instinctive rhythm that was ages old yet always new.

"Sarah," he cried, "Sarah."

"Yes, my love. I know." She surged against him, ready to accept the weight of his body when it collapsed across hers, ecstasy expanded. She sighed deeply and contentedly, and pulled his head to rest against her shoulder. Rocking him back and forth in her arms, she was unable to stop the tears of joy that flowed down her cheeks. Jim kissed them away with tender butterfly touches of his lips.

"Why did we wait so long?" she murmured. "Why weren't we doing this a long time ago?"

He gave her a puzzled look. "It was what you wanted."

"No, it wasn't. It wasn't what I wanted at all."

He shifted his position in the bed until he had a full view of her face. "You distinctly told me," he said emphatically.

"I know what I told you," she answered with a small smile, tracing the contours of his face with her fingertip. How she loved touching him. "But did you have to listen?" She gave him a light kiss on the mouth. "I think what I really wanted," she said slowly "was for you to sweep me off my feet. Tell me what a fool I was for imposing so many rules, putting forth so many objections."

His eyes swept over the long line of her body. "Well, I do seem to have you off your feet. Would it make you feel better if I said you were a fool?"

"Probably not. Though clearly I was. What made you decide to come?"

"I don't know. Maybe I was afraid you wouldn't come back."

"You thought I'd just hang out in Jamaica for the rest of my life?"

She reached up and ran her fingers through his hair and along the nape of his neck. He was hers. She could touch him when she wanted, how she wanted, and any time she wanted. How delightfully delicious to know that!

"Oh no. I knew you'd come back to St. Louis. I just wasn't sure you'd come back to me. Not in the way I wanted, anyway." He nuzzled her neck lovingly. "Sarah, you're my life, my love. Please never doubt it. I'm not saying I'll never get angry and shoot off my mouth. I seem to have a talent for that. But it has nothing to do with the depth of my feeling for you."

"Well," she said, breathing deeply, "you did manage to hide it pretty well. I wasn't sure you cared if I was around or not."

"I was only trying to comply with the rules..."

"I know," she whispered. "But I was beginning to wonder if you'd ever cared about me or whether your interest in me had only to do with Christy."

He laughed and rumpled her hair affectionately. "It's a complex situation we created, counselor. Some of it was our own doing. Some of it was beyond our control. I don't even know how to begin to explain it." His mouth some how found its way to the hollow of her throat and to a very vulnerable place at the side of her neck. Skillfully, he nuzzled and nibbled, until Sarah had to gasp.

"Please!" she giggled, rolling from him. "If we're going to talk, you'd better stop that. It's distracting!"

"Oh?" he said with a lift of his eyebrows. He reached toward her to cup her hips with his hands, pulling her body toward him, then bent to kiss her breasts with renewed ardor.

"Jim . . ." she protested feebly.

"What, love?" he said, moving his hands over the soft contours of her body in a delightfully provocative way.

"Nothing," she gasped, melting into his kiss, feeling the heat of his tongue inside her mouth. "Oh well, forget the talking for now." Her voice was slow and dreamy and she reached out to touch him, to let her hands have free rein over his lean, muscular body, knowing she was rekindling within him the same erotic stirrings she was experiencing. This time there was no need to hurry. They had the rest of the day, the rest of the night. Perhaps even the rest of their lives. She reveled in his slowly burning kisses and caresses. There was nothing mechanical in his touch. He was on fire with his need for her, and this knowledge made her glow inside and out.

Jim's hands and lips moved over her and she twisted and turned within his embrace. With Jim, there was no need to coax or command because he seemed to know what she wanted and needed before she knew it herself.

Their legs tangled, their kisses grew deeper, longer,

and Sarah knew no words to describe the delicious ache she felt as she searched his heated, hungry mouth. Moaning, she wrenched away from his kiss and let her head fall back against the pillow. Jim's hands moved to caress the dark tangled strands of hair and looked down at her with eyes glazed from love and desire. "I love you," he said.

"Me too," she whispered.

When he moved to claim her, her body throbbed with elation, a feeling of wholeness. Strong, virile, insatiable, Jim stayed with her, pleasuring her until her mind, body, and heart became inseparable, until nothing existed but the pure, sweet agony of his love-making.

As his passion deepened, she felt transported to another plane of existence. Never before had she loved like this. Spasms of pleasure crept over her involuntarily. Digging her nails into his firm flesh, she cried out from the mingled pain and pleasure. Tossing restlessly, she murmured his name. She couldn't stand it anymore, and yet she couldn't bear for him to stop.

"Stay with me, love," he commanded softly. And she did. Her body arched to accept his deep and abiding conquest.

When the fire raged too forcefully to be contained, Sarah heard his cry of surrender. Once more she held him tightly to her as the entire world swayed and jerked, coming at last to a dizzying stop.

Still somewhat dazed, she ran her hands lightly across his back and down his thighs. He trembled in response.

"I didn't think," she said huskily, "that such things

actually happened outside the covers of novels."

"What's that, love?" he asked, lips resting softly against her earlobe.

She looked at him languidly. "Why, the earth moved. Didn't you feel it? Or," she said, narrowing her hazel eyes at him suspiciously, "perhaps it's nothing new to you."

He laughed, enveloping her in a bear hug. "I felt it. I felt everything. And of course it was something new. That's just the way it is with us. I take that for granted. I told you once that when I made it to thirty without being truly in love, I doubted love existed. Well, you've proven me wrong—many times over."

"I'm glad," she murmured. "So glad. Because I love you more than it's possible. I really do. You turn me inside out and upside down..."

"Oh? That sounds exciting."

"It is. Believe me. But weren't there a few things we wanted to discuss?"

"Oh," he groaned. "Discussions. Women are never done with talking. Would you believe me if I told you I was tired?" As if to prove it, he yawned lazily.

"Can't imagine why," she said, but she didn't press the issue. Maybe there wasn't anything to talk about. They were together. They always would be. What more was there to say? As he stretched on his stomach out beside her, she leaned over to kiss the back of his neck. The red-brown hair was slightly curled, damp with the exertion of love.

Jim was the first to fall asleep. Sarah lay beside him, content and fulfilled, listening to the steady rhythm of his breath. Soon it had lulled her into near-slumber. She felt pleasantly like a small child: secure, loved, soothed by a gentle song, a soft word.

So this was love. For so long it had been a stranger in her life. Now that void was filled.

CHAPTER EIGHT

JIM AND SARAH shared a long, leisurely breakfast in the hotel's terraced dining room. No one seemed to mind that they took so long. Every other bite of food was punctuated by a deep, loving gaze or a smile. In Kingston, little notice was taken of starry-eyed lovers. In fact, the Jamaicans seemed to prefer them to the tourists who wore loud shirts and funny hats. Lovers, involved in their own world, were less demanding on the personnel.

After breakfast, Jim suggested that they go back to the beach. "Wear that red thing again," he said. "I liked it. Then we can come back up here and I'll see how you look out of it."

Sarah smiled and obstinately put on a copper-colored maillot that was every bit as enticing as the other suit had been.

"Do you ever do what you're told?" he asked, eyes flickering appreciatively over her form.

"Occasionally."

He laughed, and they spread out their towels on the beach. They held hands, rubbed suntan lotion on each other, and dozed from time to time.

"This is the life," Jim said lazily. "The morning's almost gone. Soon it's time for lunch. Sun, sleep, love. What more could we want?"

"Talk," she said, sitting up to look at him determinedly. "As I recall, you kept interrupting me. We were discussing these past weeks..."

"What about these past weeks?" he said lazily.

Sarah propped her face in her hands and sighed. "You refuse to be serious, don't you?"

"Not really. It's just that we've had so much unrelieved seriousness lately. This is much more fun."

"True," she admitted, reaching over to squeeze his hand. "Still, some things can't be ignored..."

"As I said yesterday, it's hard to know where to start. I came to Forest Park to meet you that cold, miserable rainy day. I thought, at that time, I would die if you shut me out. I was ready to do anything to make amends. I was even prepared to grovel if that's what it took."

"Grovel?" she said with a smile. "I'd never want you to do that."

"Fortunately. At least you didn't close the door completely. But, God, it was hard to be friends with you. I can't be near you without wanting to touch you, let you know that I love you. When you told me you didn't want that, weren't ready for it, I couldn't very well force myself on you."

She nodded slowly. "No. I guess I couldn't expect you to know what I wanted when I didn't know myself."

"It was fairly complex. If your objections had been less valid, I wouldn't have hesitated to overrule them and sweep you off your feet right then and there in the middle of Forest Park. But then you explained about Grant. I could see what marriage had been like for you before. You thought you knew him, but you didn't know him at all. By the time you did, you were married and it was too late. I understood, Sarah. Then I didn't want to rush you. It was hard on me, but I loved you enough to give you time and space. It seemed important. It seemed the only thing to do."

"So you just shut me out."

"I never did that," he said, smoothing her hair back from her forehead tenderly. "Wasn't it you who did that? Anyway, Sarah, I did the best I could. And, believe me, you haven't been my only problem. You know my worry and concern for Christy. Then there was the business. It's not easy with a new business venture. But there's already been progress. We've got some good contracts. I have some good people working for me, people I'm not afraid to delegate responsibility to. That's important to me, because I need time for other things. Personal things."

"I was beginning to think," she admitted, "that aviation was more important to you than I was."

His hearty laughter rang out and warmed her as

thoroughly and pleasantly as the sun's rays.

"Sarah," he said affectionately, "do you realize how perverse you are? With the energy you devote to *your* career, why on earth would you, of all people, feel threatened by mine?"

"I don't know," she mumbled, feeling foolish. "I guess I've got a double standard. It's something I'll have to work on. My perversity, as you put it. Think you can handle that?"

"I'll take it all," he said softly.

She turned slightly, angling herself into the sun. "I'm glad," she whispered, "commander."

"Ex-commander," he corrected, reaching out to place his finger on her nose.

"I know," she said, looking over at him. "I guess I just can't get that image of you in uniform out of my head. You made quite an impression on me that day you walked into my office . . ."

"Wish I'd known it at the time. But seriously, Sarah, that's been another of the complexities. Within a very short time, I lost my naval career, the hope of getting custody of Christy, and you—I thought. It was almost more than I could cope with. There are still times when I feel a sense of loss about the navy. I miss it every so often. In time, I guess it'll pass. Now that I have you and now that the business is beginning to thrive, I'm sure the adjustment period will be much easier."

"I'll do what I can to make it so," she said, feeling unaccountably shy and vulnerable. Now that Jim had opened up to her and really explained his feelings, she loved him even more. The last of her insecurities had left her. She had, from the beginning, perceived Jim as a strong man. And he was strong. Yet he was still vulnerable and human, subject to doubts, hurts, disappointments.

He gave her a long, slow stare. "That bathing suit has elevated the blood pressure of every male within thirty paces of you," he said sternly.

"How can you know that?"

"While you've been lying there with your eyes shut, I've been looking around. Besides, I know how men think."

"Gee, I thought it was a rather modest suit."

"Well," he said with mock gravity, "maybe it's not the suit. Maybe it's just you. However, the way it dips down here..." he trailed a finger between her breasts, "and rises up here..." he trailed the same finger up her thigh, "is very provocative," he concluded, his voice husky.

"Quit that," she said, giggling. "We're in public."

"We could remedy that."

"That's true. It's almost lunchtime."

"You're thinking about food," he asked, hurt.

"Well... perhaps I could be persuaded..." She dodged him artfully and jumped up from the towel. "Let's go see about lunch. Or... whatever."

"Which comes first?"

"That depends on how persuasive you are."

Back behind closed doors, Jim's arms enfolded her and his lips began their seeking, hungry assault on hers. Swaying, pressing against him, her body filled with delicious sensations, Sarah sighed audibly. "I want you," she murmured.

"Does that mean I was persuasive enough?" he whispered, licking her earlobe.

"Maybe," she purred.

He devoured her with wet, erotic kisses, and she made no protest when he moved her toward the bed. "Hungry now?" he asked, looking deeply into her eyes.

"Yes," she said thickly, "very."

Jim smiled and stretched out lazily beside her. Lunch was very late that day.

The remaining days and nights in Jamaica were an odyssey in sun, love and laughter. Sarah wished they could go on forever. But, of course, that was impossible. St. Louis was there with its snow and obligations. When the time came, she cancelled her seat on the commercial flight and flew with Jim in his Cessna.

"It could be handy," she remarked happily, "to have a man who can fly me around at whim. I could just wake up some morning and say, 'To Paris, James.'"

"But you won't," he said, grinning. "You have other priorities—as do I. It's hard to imagine you as a jet-setter, Sarah."

"Oh, I don't know," she replied, leaning back against the seat and eyeing the impressive array of controls with which Jim seemed so familiar. "I might be able to adapt."

"I like you the way you are," he said meaningfully.

Sarah returned his smile.

Maybe it was only her imagination, but the moment Jim told her they were in Missouri, Sarah felt a chill in the air. She reached for the heavy coat to slip on over her light-weight slacks and shirt. "That was a short summer," she remarked.

And when they landed on the private airstrip by Jim's hangar, it was quite evident their summer was over. It was a grim, gray Thursday morning. It seemed that no more snow had fallen, but the temperature had remained low enough that the existing snow had not melted. Ugly gray piles of it had been pushed up against curbs by the snow plows.

"Well, what now?" he asked, looking at her quizzically. They had been so insulated during their idyllic Kingston vacation that they hadn't planned beyond the moment.

"I guess," she said with slow smile, "you'd better take me to Lambert Field so I can see if my car is still there. After that, I suppose you'll be anxious to get back here and see how things went without you. Then, when I get settled in, I need to check at the office and see what's on my docket."

They exchanged glances.

"Reality," Sarah said, shaking her head.

"I expect it to be a much more pleasant reality from now on," Jim said huskily.

Sarah only smiled.

Back home, Sarah unpacked and rearranged her belongings. Suddenly it occurred to her that Christy was among the many subjects she and Jim had not discussed in Jamaica. They hadn't intentionally shut the little girl out, but, Sarah supposed, they really had been vacationing from reality. It was terrible to love the child, to want her with them, to know how miserable she was . . . and to be powerless to do anything. Now that they were home, however, she knew they would have to settle down and deal with the problem realistically.

Before they had had time to discuss Christy, however, fate intervened. Sarah spent the next evening at Jim's. As she was preparing dinner, the telephone rang.

Jim answered it in another room, then came into the kitchen. His expression was grim. "I have to go get Christy. Joy says it's all right for me to have her a few days early."

"Joy called?" Sarah asked.

"Christy did. She was practically beside herself. She was crying, and said they were going to move far away and that she might never get to see me ever, ever again. I don't know what's going on."

"Okay, run get her," Sarah said quietly. "I'll finish dinner. There's plenty for all of us."

Jim took Sarah in his arms and held her to him, the brief embrace and kiss giving her a warm afterglow of pleasure. This evening, before she had started dinner, he had already proven to her that being back in cold St. Louis hadn't put a freeze on his ardor . . . and that lovemaking was every bit as satisfactory here as it had been in Jamaica.

She looked into his eyes and remembered the most recent moments of shared passion, the way it had built slowly to an almost unbearable pitch. The two of them seemed to blend emotionally, physically, sensually— all ways. Over and over again, within his arms, she found all she ever needed to know of love and desire. They shared an almost magical intensity of passion that transcended time and place. To Sarah, it would never matter where or when, just so long as it was Jim. Pulling away from him, she smiled and raised her lips for a kiss.

"See you soon," Jim said. And then he was gone, leaving the memory of his warm lips clinging sweetly to her own.

When he returned with Christy, her face tear-stained, Sarah had dinner ready.

Jim gave her a warning glance, and Sarah didn't ask questions. By keeping up a stream of chatter, she was able to coax a few smiles from the child, who did manage to eat a few bites.

When Christy left the room, Jim whispered, "Can we talk about this. You'll spend the night, won't you? Or at least stick around until after she's gone to bed?"

Sarah nodded her acceptance.

Later, when Christy had been tucked in for the night, Sarah approached Jim in the living room. His features were taut with tension and a cigarette glowed from between his fingers.

She sat down beside him and remarked, "You didn't smoke once when we were in Jamaica."

The tension temporarily eased from his face and he smiled at her. "I had better things to do," he said huskily.

"Mmm," Sarah said, returning his smile. "But Jim, tell me. What's the story with Christy?"

He took a deep pull on the cigarette. "Joy had already left when I got there. Otherwise, I'm sure we'd have had a terrible row. Maybe it's just as well I'll have a chance to cool down.

"There was a realtor's FOR SALE sign on the front

lawn," he continued. "A babysitter was there with Christy. The kid was close to hysterics, and the sitter didn't know what to do. I got Christy calmed down, and we took the sitter home. Between the two of them, I managed to piece the story together. Apparently, Joy has decided to marry again. The man's name is Yves; I didn't get the last name. Joy met him through her work. Apparently, he's got quite a name in the world of interior design. I gather Christy isn't totally wild about him, but that isn't the main problem. This man is based in Europe. He was only here on a promotional tour. His main office is in Paris. From what Christy says, he intends to keep it that way, and Joy isn't objecting. The plan is to move to France . . . the three of them."

"Oh, Jim, *no*."

"Oh yes. She's off with him now in New York at some products' exhibition, which was why she allowed Christy to come tonight. But when she gets back, we'll have it out. She's not taking my child out of the country. No way."

Sarah didn't reply. There wasn't much she could say. As much as she hated the idea, she strongly suspected Joy would do exactly as she pleased—and that Jim would have about as much power to do anything about it as he had had all along.

In the end, Sarah spent the night. But after that, she didn't see Jim and Christy for several days. She wanted to give them time together, to let Jim soothe the child in his own way.

"You aren't dropping out of my life forever, are you?" he chided her on the phone.

"Just try and get rid of me!" she returned. "I'll be by on Sunday. Let's just plan a nice day and let the future take care of itself."

"I'm afraid it can't be that way, love. I'll have to take action of some sort."

"Just don't be hasty, Jim. Let's plan it out together."

"Sure thing. I love you."

"And I love you, Jim."

Sarah felt the stirrings of dread in her heart as she hung up the phone. None of this would be happening if she had won the hearing. As she had a thousand times before, she went over every detail in her mind, trying to think of something she could have done differently. Did Jim have similar thoughts?

Sunday did prove a pleasant day, but they couldn't shake a pervasive feeling of doom. While Christy's attention was focused raptly on a television cartoon show, Jim sat next to Sarah on the couch, pulling her close. He kissed her tenderly, but she saw the passion in his eyes.

"I need you," he whispered. "You stayed away too long."

In answer, Sarah kissed him deeply, leaving little doubt of her own burning desire. One look, one touch. That was all it seemed to take, she thought, to become heady with longing.

The sound of a car pulling up out front took Christy's attention from the television program. "That sounds like Mother's car," she said, her eyes clouding.

Jim looked at his watch and shook his head in

disgust. "She's not supposed to be here for two hours yet. I suppose she decided that since I picked you up early, she's taking you back early."

"Daddy, please . . ."

"Don't start it, Christy. Just let me handle this and do the best I can." Anxiety made his tone sharper than he realized, and the child looked to Sarah for sympathy.

Sarah reached out to pull Christy onto her lap. "Don't worry, hon. He's not mad at you, he's just worried."

The doorbell sounded and Jim went to open the door. Joy stood on the doorstep, glacially elegant in a slim black coat.

Without invitation she entered, her eyes focusing on Sarah. Assessing Sarah's rumpled appearance, Joy smiled. "My, what a cozy domestic scene. I'm surprised to see you here, Ms. Harbison. I gather you have more than a casual interest in your . . . client. Not that I entirely blame you. Jim is an attractive man. There are times when I . . . well, enough of that." Joy's cool eyes roved over Jim in a possessive, knowing way.

Sarah felt her pulse rise.

"We should discuss things, Joy," Jim said coolly, ignoring her comments. "Is your fiancé in the car? Why not have him come in? There's nothing I have to say he can't hear."

"Oh my, that sounds ominous," she said. "But actually, Yves isn't with me. How did you know we were engaged? I just dropped him off at his hotel. Let me have a seat."

She slid gracefully into a chair, crossed her shapely legs, and lit a cigarette in one deft motion. "Perhaps you should go to your room, Christy, and pick up your things. This won't take long."

Instead of obeying passively, Christy rooted herself more firmly on Sarah's lap. She glared at her mother. "I won't go. I hate Yves. I hate Paris. I hate Europe. And I hate . . ."

"Christy," Sarah warned softly, placing a restraining finger across the child's lips. "Daddy said for you to let him handle this. Now, go do what your mother said."

"No," Christy said defiantly. "I want to stay here. I won't go. I won't."

Her piping, childish voice rose higher with every syllable.

Joy gave her a furious look. "Christina," she snapped, "go to your room. This is a time for adults to talk. Go play with your dolls."

"I hate my dolls."

"Then play with something you don't hate. But *go.* And *now.*"

Sarah looked at Jim questioningly.

Putting an arm around her shoulders, he said, "Stay here. You're a part of this. Christy, be a good girl and go to your room. One of us will come in there with you in just a few minutes."

Christy slowly unfolded herself and climbed off Sarah's lap. Sulkily, she crossed the room.

Sarah didn't blame her. Christy might be very young, but she knew her future was being discussed. It was only natural that she wanted to stay.

"You aren't moving her to Europe, Joy," Jim said the moment Christy was out of the room. "I won't let that happen."

Through a veil of blue smoke, Joy smiled. "Oh? And how exactly do you intend to stop me?"

"With a court order, if necessary. You know the custody agreement guarantees me regular visitation rights. You can't take her out of the country without my permission."

"We'll have the custody arrangements modified, Jim. I understand that's quite standard."

Sarah knew Joy was right. It wasn't uncommon to alter the specifics of visitation rights. The most Jim could hope for would be the right to have Christy during the summers.

"I'll fight you, Joy," Jim said bitterly. "But, Joy, tell me something. Just answer one question. Why?"

"Why what?" she asked.

"Why do this to Christy and me? Can't you see how unhappy she is? It's apparent you really don't have the time and patience to deal with her. I realize you love her, Joy. But isn't it possible that motherhood isn't your primary interest right now?"

Joy was silent. Instead of looking at Jim, she slowly appraised Sarah. Sarah met her eyes with a calmness she didn't feel.

"Is motherhood Ms. Harbison's primary interest?" Joy hissed. "How convenient to have a lover, attorney, and housemother all in one."

"I won't have you insult Sarah," Jim said, his face a mask. "And furthermore . . ."

Sarah placed a restraining hand on his arm. "Let

her say what she wants. It doesn't matter. I'm not at issue here. Christy is."

"You see?" Joy said with a brittle laugh. "Better keep this one. She's smarter than you are. Now, you've jumped to some hasty conclusions. You seem to assume that I'm taking Christy to Paris to live with Yves and me."

Sarah's spine stiffened, and she looked at Joy warily.

"Aren't you?" Jim asked. "That's what she'd been told."

"I had hoped we could talk reasonably, Jim. Is that going to be possible? We did, between us, bring this child into the world. Let's talk about what's best for her."

A look of utter skepticism crossed Jim's handsome features. "Then talk, Joy," he said simply.

"Well, as you've surmised, taking her with us was what I had planned. It's what I want. But Christina's been impossible since the issue was broached. I want Christy with me. I want that more than anything. That's why I fought your custody appeal. It hurt to have Christy say she wanted to live with you, but I thought it was just a stage she was going through. I thought she'd get over it. Whether or not you believe this, I almost gave up the idea of marrying Yves because Christy was so opposed. But in the end I couldn't do that, Jim. And Christy hasn't adjusted. In fact, she's gotten worse. There isn't a day goes by but that she lets me know how much she'd rather be here with you. It hurts, but there it is. I know that if I give up Yves, give up the chance to live in Paris,

I'll still hear her complaints. You see how she is with me. She was ready to say she hated me when Ms. Harbison stopped her."

"Call me Sarah," Sarah said firmly. She glanced at Jim, who seemed dazed.

"Let me get this straight," he said slowly, deliberately. "Are you trying to tell me that you'll let Christy stay here with me?"

"That's what I'm saying. You can't know how it breaks my heart. But the time has come when I have to put her happiness above my own. If she objects so violently to being with me, then I'll have to give her up. There it is. I don't know what else to do. Perhaps when she's older and better able to understand, things will be different. Maybe then she won't hate me."

A tear rolled down Joy's cheek. Sarah wasn't impressed. She was familiar with the woman's acting talents. The way Sarah saw it, Joy wanted a new life and the child was in the way. Especially now that she was making such a fuss. Joy wanted to be free to start a new life, and dealing with a pre-schooler's emotional traumas would cut into that freedom.

Sarah looked at Jim. His expression registered the same skepticism; in fact, he looked as though he was about ready to tell Joy off. Catching his eye, Sarah shook her head ever so slightly. Let her have her say, she thought. Getting Christy is more important than gaining a triumph over Joy.

Jim gave Sarah a look filled with warmth. Imperceptibly, he nodded, then moved his gaze to his former wife. "You know you don't have to ask, Joy. You know I want her. She can stay now, or she can come when you're ready to move. Just let me know. I'll come get all her things . . ."

Joy relaxed visibly. "Good. I was sure you'd understand. I'd like to take her back with me tonight so I can explain it to her in my own way."

Jim nodded. "That's fine," he said. "When shall I come get her, then?"

"In one week. Is that okay with you?"

"It's fine."

Joy had already started to rise when Sarah spoke. "Jim, don't jump into this too quickly," she warned. "There are still some things to be worked out."

He looked at her in surprise.

Noting this, Joy laughed. "We may have a complication, Jim. Ms. Harbison . . . Sarah obviously isn't keen on dealing with Christy permanently. A weekend here and there is not the same as full-time."

Sarah appraised her coolly. "That is not the problem," she said. "Nothing would please me more than to have Christy's company more often. But as a lawyer, I think we'd better take this discussion a step further. If you really want what's best for your child, then make this change of custody official. I can start the proceedings tomorrow and have the papers ready to be signed and notarized before you leave for Europe. By tomorrow, if need be."

"Papers?" Joy's eyebrows arched perceptibly. "I'm afraid I don't understand."

"Jim needs to know that you won't be taking Christina back should you decide to return from Europe. You might not like living abroad. The marriage might fail. You and your husband both might decide to return to the States. Christy needs a stable environment. If you're convinced her happiness lies in being with her father, then you surely won't hesitate to make his primary custody legal."

"But I'd want to see her sometimes," Joy insisted.

"It was never my intention to prevent that," Jim said softly. "How about it, Joy?"

For the first time, Joy looked vulnerable as she bent her fair head in a reluctant nod of agreement.

Jim stood up, his dark eyes dancing with pleasure. "Would you like something to drink, Joy, while I go talk to our daughter and help her get ready?"

"Please," she said gratefully.

"I'll get it," Sarah offered. "You go see to Christy."

A few minutes later a jubilant father and daughter emerged from the pink and white room.

Christy ran to Sarah and hugged her fiercely. "When I come back, Sarah, I get to *stay*. Did you know that?"

"Yes, sweetheart!"

"And will you be here?"

"We'll see. Good night, Christy love. Be nice to your mother. This isn't easy for her."

When the door closed behind them, Jim and Sarah faced each other.

"I want to ask you the same question Christy did, Sarah. Will you be here? I want you to marry me as soon as possible. I want us to be a family in the right way, the best way."

Sarah waited for the burst of happiness to sail through her heart. Wasn't this everything she'd wanted? Everything she'd dreamed of? But something prevented it. Yes, she wanted to share the jubilation she'd seen on Jim's face, on Christy's. And yet, Joy's ugly words haunted her. *How convenient to have a lover, attorney, and housemother all in one.* Hadn't she thought much the same thing herself at one time?

"Sarah," Jim said, sinking onto the couch beside her. "Am I rushing you? Pushing things? I want to give you all the time and space you need, darling, but I so much want you with me. If you're having second thoughts about taking on so much responsibility—a ready-made family—I don't blame you. Just talk to me, Sarah. Tell me how you feel."

"You know I don't think of Christy as a ready-made anything. I'd love her even if she wasn't yours. She's a person all her own. And a very dear little person. But..."

"But *what*, love?"

"You haven't mentioned marriage before. Are you sure there isn't some truth in what Joy says? That suddenly it's very...convenient?"

Jim whistled softly. "Joy knows how to get to a person, doesn't she? Right for the jugular. A few minutes in her company and we're doubting each other all over again. Look at me, Sarah."

Sarah raised her eyes to his deep brown ones, which were filled with love.

"This past week has been crazy. No sooner had we returned from Jamaica than I was hit with the threat of losing Christy completely. Maybe I never actually said, 'Marry me.' But you surely know that's what I meant. It's what I always intended...and just as soon as you'd agree. Maybe I was waiting for you to tell me you were ready."

Sarah laughed. "Even in these advanced times, it is still customary for the man to propose."

"Yes, but you were the one with all the objections," he pointed out.

Sarah couldn't argue with that. "Then let's run this through one more time," she said, grinning.

"Counselor, really."

"Please?"

"All right. But first, thanks for pinning Joy down and making this legal. I was so overjoyed at the prospect of having Christy that I didn't think. Thank goodness you did."

"Roger told you I was a good lawyer."

"Roger is halfway in love with you. He must be; if he isn't, he's a fool."

"Oh, stop. He isn't. But anyway, that has nothing to do with it." Sarah looked at him. "You don't think I'm a good lawyer?"

He smiled at her, his dark eyes dancing with mischief. "I think you're good at everything, darling. But then, I'm prejudiced. I'm completely in love with you."

"That's nice, but we still have things to discuss."

He sighed. "We always do."

"You said I'm good at everything. Does that include being a mother? Your little girl deserves the best."

"You are the best."

"And you think I can manage you, her, and my career?"

"Why not?"

"I'll try. That's all I can promise."

"That's good enough."

"Are you going to want more kids?"

He looked at her in open-mouthed amazement. "Good Lord, Sarah. The next thing I know, you'll be wanting to draw up a prenuptial agreement."

She gave him a slow smile. "Just answer the question, please."

"Yes, I'd like to have more kids," he said, squaring his shoulders and looking her directly in the eyes. "But if you don't, I won't force the issue. If I have you and Christy, I won't push my luck. But . . . do you?"

"Yes," she said simply. "And I'm not getting any younger. I think we'd better get started."

Jim's eyes widened in surprise as she slowly unbuttoned her blouse.

Within minutes, they were in Jim's room tumbling around on the bed, giggling like teenagers as they undressed each other.

"I love how we laugh when we make love," Sarah whispered.

"I know," said Jim, running his hand down her thigh. "I hate sad sex."

Sarah giggled until he closed his mouth over hers. They made love fully, completely, taking pleasure in each movement, each caress.

Afterward, when their breathing had returned to normal and tumult was replaced with peace, Jim looked down at her, narrowing his eyes till the crinkles at the corners deepened. "You're pregnant," he announced.

Reaching up to rumple his hair, Sarah smiled. "How can you possibly know that?"

Laughing, he fell back onto the bed. "Because you aren't the only one who's good at everything. When I set out to do something, I do it right the first time. I used to be a naval commander, you know."

Sarah threw a pillow at him. Never had she felt so happy. Everything she wanted was to be hers. Who said fairy-tale endings didn't exist?

Sighing, she relaxed back into his arms.

"Happy, darling?" he murmured.

"Oh, yes," she whispered. "Oh, yes."

With that he reached over and flicked off the light.

WATCH FOR 6 NEW TITLES EVERY MONTH!

All of the above titles are $1.75 per copy except where noted

SK-41a

WHAT READERS SAY ABOUT
SECOND CHANCE AT LOVE BOOKS